"Going somewhere, Athena?"

Her breath hitched in her lungs as every nerve receptor in her body screamed in alarm.

Alexios!

How did he know she was here?

She spun around, incensed. Because if he knew she was here, he must surely know why, and she was suddenly, terribly, afraid. His jaw was set, his eyes were unrepentant, and they scanned her now, as if looking for evidence, taking inventory of any changes. There weren't any, not that anyone else might notice, though she'd felt her jeans grow more snug just lately, the beginnings of a baby bump.

"We need to talk."

"I've got nothing to say to you," she said.

"No?" His eyes flicked up to the brass plate near the door, to the name of the doctor in obstetrics. "You didn't think I might be interested to hear that you're pregnant with my child?"

One Night With Consequences

When one night...leads to pregnancy!

When succumbing to a night of unbridled desire, it's impossible to think past the morning after!

But with the sheets barely settled, that little blue line appears on the pregnancy test, and it doesn't take long to realize that one night of white-hot passion has turned into a lifetime of consequences!

Only one question remains:

How do you tell a man you've just met that you're about to share more than just his bed?

Find out in:

A Baby to Bind His Bride by Caitlin Crews

Claiming His Nine-Month Consequence
by Jennie Lucas

Contracted for the Petrakis Heir by Annie West

Consequence of His Revenge by Dani Collins

Princess's Pregnancy Secret by Natalie Anderson

The Sheikh's Shock Child by Susan Stephens

The Italian's One-Night Consequence
by Cathy Williams

Princess's Nine-Month Secret by Kate Hewitt

Look for more One Night With Consequences coming soon!

Trish Morey

CONSEQUENCE OF THE GREEK'S REVENGE

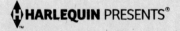
HARLEQUIN PRESENTS®

Recycling programs for this product may not exist in your area.

ISBN-13: 978-1-335-50472-2

Consequence of the Greek's Revenge

First North American publication 2018

Copyright © 2018 by Trish Morey

Printed in U.S.A.

www.Harlequin.com

Trish Morey always fancied herself a writer—so why she became a chartered accountant is anyone's guess! But once she'd found her true calling there was no turning back. Mother of four budding heroines and wife to one true-life hero, Trish lives in an idyllic region of South Australia. Is it any wonder she believes in happily-ever-afters?

Find her at trishmorey.com or Facebook.com/trish.morey.

Books by Trish Morey

Harlequin Presents

A Price Worth Paying?
Bartering Her Innocence
The Heir from Nowhere
His Prisoner in Paradise
His Mistress for a Million

Desert Brothers

Duty and the Beast
The Sheikh's Last Gamble
Captive of Kadar

Visit the Author Profile page at Harlequin.com for more titles.

Thank you, dear reader.

It's good to be back.

CHAPTER ONE

Stavros Nikolides was dead.

Alexios Kyriakos balled his hands into fists as he read the online news report. The man his father had looked up to and trusted like no other, the man who had subsequently betrayed him and left him broken and shattered, had suffered a massive heart attack while partying on his yacht, his life snuffed out between a magnum of champagne and his bikini-clad mistress.

Dead.

It should be enough.

He stood, unable to digest the news sitting down, the muscles in his long legs itching for action, and carrying him to the wall of glass that looked out across the city of Athens to the Acropolis where the ruins of the Parthenon baked under a relentlessly hot Greek sun.

The gods had exacted their revenge.

It *should* be enough.

Except that it wasn't.

Instead Alexios felt cheated. Denied the opportunity to yank Stavros's diamond-encrusted life out from beneath him. Denied the opportunity to balance the scales on his own terms, when vengeance had been so damned close he could taste it.

Where was the revenge he'd promised his father on his deathbed? Where was the levelling of the score he'd worked towards these last ten years? He'd never once begged the gods to solve his problems. He'd stood on his own two feet and looked after himself from day one. Why now had they intervened and stolen the vengeance he had worked so hard for?

He stared up at the mount, teeming with sweltering tourists, as if the answer lay there, amidst the ruins of the Parthenon and the Temple of Athena Nike. And a switch flicked in his head.

Athena.

He strode back to the desk, scrolling down the report, pausing when he came to the two photographs. One grainy file shot of her in a string bikini draped on a yacht anchored off the Amalfi Coast, the other of her wearing dark glasses and a pinched expression as she pushed past the cameras and microphones jostling for a picture and a reaction outside the hospital morgue where her father's body had been taken.

Athena Nikolides. Twenty-seven-year-old product of Stavros's short-lived marriage to an Australian model turned actress, and now no doubt heiress to a fortune—a fortune her father had stolen from anyone and everyone he could steal from.

Athena Nikolides.

With her mother's stunning looks and her father's ill-gotten fortune.

There was his revenge.

CHAPTER TWO

ATHENA SAT NUMBLY in a café in Thera, barely registering the coffee she'd ordered set before her, let alone the sprawling sea-filled caldera of Santorini far below or the way its surface sparkled like jewels under a September sun that still packed a punch.

It was the three cruise ships that lay anchored that held her gaze, or, rather, their tenders, busy like bees ferrying passengers back to their vessels after a day riding donkeys up the steep steps and wandering the cobbled steps of the towns clinging to the cliff's edge. Idly she watched the tiny boats come and go, their movements vaguely therapeutic.

She took a long breath of the clean salt air, and let it out slowly, feeling the tension in her shoulders and neck dissipate with the steady rhythm of their to-ing and fro-ing, easing the dull ache in her head she'd had ever since leaving the sterile steel and concrete offices of her father's lawyers in Athens.

It was the shock, she knew. The shock, and the strain of trying to follow a legal conversation delivered in rapid-fire Greek, that had made her head spin. Her conversational skills might have been enough to get her through her university studies, but they were no match for the full-on onslaught of legalese she'd had to interpret, and the certainty that she must have got it wrong.

It wasn't until she'd held up one hand and appealed to them that she didn't understand, that nothing made sense, that one of them had taken pity on her, and uttered the words in English. 'It's quite simple, Athena, your father left it all to you. Everything he owned. Every last euro.'

And even delivered in English, that had made the least sense of all.

She shook her head, just as she'd shaken her head then, still battling to come to terms with a morning that defied logic and had left her reeling.

She'd entered the offices confused about why she'd even been summoned, only to exit it one hour later baffled, because suddenly she was one of the richest women in Greece. The estranged father who'd disinherited her when she was in her teens had left it all to her, his fortune, a home in Athens, a super-yacht complete with helicopter, and then the jewel in the crown, the Aegean island of Argos.

Every last bit of his fortune left to her.

And she'd had no idea.

She tossed back her coffee as a string of donkeys led by a man with a leathered face clip-clopped lethargically by, the animals worn out from ferrying cruise-ship passengers up and down the cobbled path to the crater's edge. It was impossible not to feel for the creatures, but there was good reason Santorini attracted so many visitors. The stark beauty of the ring of islands and its seemingly bottomless blue crater, the dark looming cliffs of ancient volcanic ash with their white buildings around the crater's rim like icing on a cake. Along with the famous sunsets.

Athena loved it for all those reasons and more, for its rich ancient history and for the elemental power of the weather, the wind so wild at times, it threatened to hurl you from the crater's edge. As she felt now. Tossed by the winds of fortune.

She'd been so right to come.

She felt real here. Humbled.

Besides, where else would she go?

Back to Melbourne where she'd grown up

after her parents had divorced, where all her school friends were, or to the tiny dot of a village from where her father had come, that she remembered only one time visiting as a child? She could go to either, but she would be known. Friends in Melbourne. Family in the village to welcome their long-lost relative. Her aunts and uncles and cousins many times removed. There would be hugs and tears and concern for how she was coping, and that would be lovely, but there would be no room to think.

And after this morning's revelations, more than ever, she needed to think.

Whereas she could breathe here, on this magical island in the midst of the Aegean. She could think. And right now she desperately needed to do both.

'May I?'

It was the voice that compelled her to look up, rather than just wave her agreement to share her table as she usually would, the voice that punctuated the hubbub of the chatter around her. Rich and thick, like the grounds in the bottom of her tiny coffee cup, and so deep she could almost feel its vibrations. A voice that suited him, she discovered a moment later. *Immaculate* was the word that sprang first into her mind. Tall and dark, with chiselled jaw and thick dark hair closely swept back at the sides, longer and sculpted in waves at the top.

But it was his eyes that hers had to return to for a second look. Dark and long-lashed, they held too much to be the eyes of someone simply looking for a place to sip their coffee, and an electric jolt zapped down her spine.

His lips turned up into a smile and her brain kicked back in.

'Oh, yes, of course.'

He curled his long frame onto the stool alongside her, the outside of his leg brushing hers, a kiss of sudden heat that made her jump. She pulled her legs away, took a calming breath.

'You like your coffee strong.'

It wasn't a question.

She nodded without looking up, her fingers cradling the tiny cup. 'It helps me think.'

'Thinking is good,' he said, taking a sip of his own coffee before adding, 'But you also need to find something that makes you smile.'

She looked across at him quizzically. 'Excuse me, but do I know you?'

'Do I need to know you to know you look sad? Pensive? Like you have the weight of the world on your shoulders?'

She couldn't speak. She couldn't believe

anyone was talking to her this way, let alone a stranger.

'No,' he said into the silence between them, swirling his own coffee in his big hand. Long tapered fingers, she noticed, dusted with tiny dark hairs and finished with neatly trimmed nails. 'We've never met,' he said, without taking his dark eyes from hers. 'There is no way I would have forgotten, if we had.'

His eyes and words combined so it felt like a velvet glove stroking its way down her spine, and it was so long since she'd felt anything close to a spark of attraction, an eternity it seemed, that she could almost forgive him for initiating a conversation no stranger had a right to.

And for all she knew there should be no reason to stay and talk, her coffee finished, for some reason she was tempted to linger, and experience these foreign feelings just that bit longer.

'My name is Alexios,' he offered, and she knew he was in no rush to go anywhere in a hurry either.

'Athena,' she said.

'Ah. Goddess of wisdom and craft.'

She smiled. 'Not to mention goddess of war.'

He conceded her point with a tilt of his

head, his dark hair glossy under the sun's light. 'True enough, yet possessing a calm temperament and moving slowly to anger, and then only to fight for just causes.'

'You know your ancient Greek mythology,' she said, impressed.

He shrugged. 'I am Greek,' he said, confirming what she'd suspected, even though they'd been speaking in English. 'It would be ignorant of me to be unaware of my heritage.'

'And so, Alexios—' She thought for a moment. 'That would make you a defender of mankind, am I right?'

He smiled, and again she was taken aback by how good-looking he was when he smiled, his lips framed by his shadowed face, darker in the cleft of his jaw, while the unbuttoned neck of his shirt shifted softly in the breeze, drawing her eyes further south, the stark white linen contrasting with the slice of olive skin of his throat and chest.

'The goddess of war and the defender of mankind,' he said. 'The world would be a safer place in our joint hands, don't you think?'

And suddenly she realised she'd been staring at him and she looked hastily away, knowing he was flirting with her, and finding herself enjoying it, even if she wasn't sure how to respond. She didn't do flirting. It felt like for ever since she'd felt carefree enough and interested enough to make a first move, let alone a second. 'I don't know about that.'

A couple squeezed past then, an American and his wife, fresh from a cruise ship and full of excited chatter at the view, and she took advantage of the distraction to shift her chair and turn her attention out over the caldera again, feigning interest in the sideways sway of the cruise ships at anchor, and the steady movement of tenders to and fro. She was nothing more than a temporary diversion in her visitor's day. He'd soon finish his coffee and move on.

'I have a problem,' he said, refusing to cooperate with her expectations. 'Maybe the woman named for the goddess of wisdom could help me.'

She looked back at him, setting her eyes to narrow, suddenly suspicious. 'I don't see how.'

'You see, soon the sun will set on the most romantic island in the world, and I am eating alone.'

'And what does that have to do with me?'

'You could help me, very much, if you would agree to dine with me.'

She sighed, taking one last look over the

sparkling waters of the caldera, feeling disappointed now. Conversation with a stranger who made her skin tingle over a shared table was one thing, dinner was another. She'd heard stories about the men who preyed on lonely women promising them all kinds of romance, and attraction was just the kind of thing that would tempt a woman to let down her guard.

And after this morning's stunning revelations, she had more reason than ever to be wary. He couldn't know. Nobody outside that office could possibly know, but she'd been warned to be careful, given her inheritance, and that just meant being more careful than ever.

'I'm sorry. I'm not looking for a gigolo. Maybe you should advertise your...' she allowed her eyes to roam purposefully over the olive-skinned vee of his chest '...*problem*, somewhere else.'

He leaned back in his chair and laughed, his shirt pulled taut over a sculpted chest so she could see the dark circles and the hard nubs of his nipples, and she could almost smell the testosterone rolling off him in waves. 'Nobody has ever called me a gigolo before.'

She forced her eyes back to his. He was attractive. Sexy. What of it? 'No? You don't make a habit of picking up sad-and-lonely-looking women in bars here on Santorini?'

'Only the very beautiful ones.'

It was her turn to laugh. She couldn't help it. It was a ridiculous conversation and the man was outrageous, but at the same time he was like a breath of fresh air in her out-of-kilter world. She couldn't remember the last time she'd laughed.

He was smiling now himself. 'You see? You should laugh more. You are even more beautiful when you laugh.'

She could say the same about him. His smile lines complemented without weakening the hard angles of his jaw, the harsh line of his mouth had softened, his lips turned up. Warmer.

And his eyes—his eyes looked at her as if he knew her. It was disconcerting. She blinked that thought away. Nobody knew who she was. Nobody knew she was here. She'd left the lawyer's offices and headed straight to her apartment to pack a carry bag, booking a flight in the taxi on the way to the airport.

'Well?' he said. 'What's it to be? Dinner with me or a night alone and morose and a lifetime spent regretting it?'

'You're very sure of yourself.'

'I'm very sure of the fact I want to have dinner with you. I want to get to know you better.'

'Why?'

'Because I have a feeling I'm going to like what I discover. Very much.'

She shook her head. It was ridiculous to feel half tempted. She didn't do blind dates. She didn't let herself get picked up in cafés. She didn't let herself get picked up, period. And that little voice in her head asking her why not just this one time could just get back in its box and shut up, especially given the lawyers' warnings.

Except the voice in her head was conspiring with Alexios's pleading dark chocolate eyes to resist arrest. Why shouldn't she have dinner with this man? it argued. What was wrong with feeling attracted to him and actually acting on it? Nobody knew who she was, and even if people had seen photos of her in the press, she was no household name. People might think she looked familiar, but she hadn't been interesting or scandalous enough to become common paparazzi fodder—not for a long time.

After the undisciplined years of her late teens, she'd made sure of that. She'd been cautious. Responsible. Determined to keep out of the public eye as much as possible.

Which meant not taking unnecessary risks, however good-looking those risks might be.

'No,' she said finally, common sense winning over recklessness, not letting him argue further when he raised one hand as if to protest. 'I'm afraid not. Thanks for the conversation. It's been…'

'Tempting?'

'Interesting.' Although she knew his word was far closer to the truth.

Someone brushed quickly behind her before moving away—a waiter gathering cups and plates, she presumed—so she had to wait a few moments until she could push her chair back. 'It's been lovely chatting. Have a pleasant evening.' And then she reached beside her to where she'd left her bags. Except there was only one there. She blinked, checking on the floor under and around the chair.

'What is it?' he asked.

'My handbag,' she said. 'It's gone.' She scanned the café, saw a man scooting between the tables towards the exit, the white strap of her shoulder bag trailing under the crook of his arm, and felt the sickening realisation that it hadn't been a waiter or even a customer brushing past behind her, but a thief. He glimpsed back over his shoulder as if checking he'd made a clean getaway, guilt written all over his profile, and she was on her feet, pointing. 'Stop!' she cried, before appealing to the startled restaurant patrons, 'That man's stolen my bag. Someone stop him!'

'Wait here,' said Alexios, with a comforting hand to her shoulder and already off in pursuit, heads of patrons turning as he cut a swathe through the tables.

The waiter stood back for Alexios before he wove his way across to her, full of apologies and consolation. 'Let me get you another coffee,' he offered.

'Not coffee,' she said, not needing it. Her heart was already beating wildly in her chest. It needed no more stimulation. Her passport and her purse were in that bag. The thief had a head start on Alexios. If he disappeared amidst the alleyways of Thera and if she lost it…

The waiter nodded, only to return with sparkling water instead, and a tiny ouzo, 'To calm your nerves', while an American woman at the next table leaned over to pat her on the arm, tut-tutting about thieves who preyed on tourists, and hoping that Athena's husband would get her handbag back.

She didn't have the heart to tell the woman the truth, that they had never met before today. Because the second Alexios had disappeared, another unpalatable possibility had already wiggled its way into her consciousness, that her would-be rescuer and thief had been working together, one to distract her with compliments and meaningless conversation, while the other worked out the best time to strike. She'd assumed he was some kind of gigolo when all the time he was more likely some kind of common thief.

A devastatingly handsome, charming thief. More fool her.

The seconds ticked by, feeling like minutes, all the smooth-talking compliments he'd given coming back to haunt her, mocking her. He'd called her beautiful and she'd been charmed stupid because of it. And suddenly she couldn't sit there any more. Why was she waiting for a stranger to return with her purse? She should be going to the police.

The waiter waved aside the bill when she promised to return, when there was a commotion at the door, followed by applause and cheers, and there, standing in the doorway, was Alexios, breathing hard and holding her bag.

Relief surged like a wave over her. Never had she seen a more welcome sight. 'You caught him?'

'I did,' he said, handing her the bag. 'The boy won't be bothering anyone around here again.'

More cheers rose from the patrons and Alexios was hailed a hero while Athena opened her bag to check her passport and purse were still there. 'I was just about to go to the police. Should we report it anyway, in case he tries again?'

'He didn't have time to open it, let alone steal anything,' Alexios assured her. 'And after the talking-to I gave him, I'm sure he won't be trying that again any time soon.'

'Thank you,' she said, peeling off some bills to pay for their coffees. 'My passport and my credit cards are in here. I don't know how to repay you.'

He smiled. 'That's hardly necessary. Though, if you insist, my invitation still stands to come to dine with me, if you care to change your mind?'

Her eyelids closed on a slow blink. The man had just rescued her handbag and she felt a flush of guilt for thinking Alexios might be working alongside the thief. And after he had proven himself trustworthy by catching up with the thief who had stolen her bag, it would be churlish to refuse dinner with him now, surely?

Besides, just for once it was nice to be able to give into temptation and not feel guilty about it. What possible harm could it do?

Her smile told him all he needed to know. He was already smiling himself before she uttered the words, 'It would be my pleasure. Of course I'll have dinner with you.'

CHAPTER THREE

HE HAD HER.

He'd never doubted it would work, of course. He'd expected her to refuse his advances, but he'd been prepared for that. What better way to secure her agreement than to make her believe she owed him? It had all gone off with domino simplicity, and now the blood in his veins pumped with new purpose, his plan unfolding as he led her through the winding paths and towards the table for two he'd prearranged that would give the best view of the sunset.

'Santorini is my favourite Greek island,' he said, as they strolled together through the labyrinthine paths. There was no need to rush. Sunset was still some time away, despite the jockeying already going on for positions. 'Perhaps my favourite place in the world.'

'Mine too,' she said.

'Is that so? Then we have something in

common. This is a good place to start, don't you think?'

She smiled in a way that told him she was amused rather than impressed. 'I'm sure it's a favourite for many people in the world.'

'True,' he conceded, knowing he still had work to do. She'd agreed to dinner but she was still wavering, he could see, still cautious. But she'd come around. It wasn't as if it were a chore to charm her. He'd been speaking the truth to her over coffee. When she smiled, her face came alight, her surprisingly blue eyes dancing, and the most surprising discovery of all—dimples in her cheeks either side of her lush mouth, that turned classically beautiful into bewitching.

And then there was the way she moved. Wearing a cute nineteen-fifties-inspired sundress, with wide shoulders and full skirt all cinched in at the waist to accentuate the slim form that lay beneath, she moved with model grace, the sway of her hips sending the skirt of her dress in a seductive motion that had him already itching to peel it off.

No, it would be no hardship bedding her. No hardship at all. And before she knew it, she'd be so busy luxuriating in the glow of the loved, he'd relieve her of her fortune without her even noticing.

And by the time she did, revenge would be his.

It was perfect.

The sun was slipping lower in the sky, couples and groups of tourists already staking their claim for what they thought the best vantage point from which to witness the sun dipping into the sea in all its molten glory.

He made small talk as they wended their way through the town, keeping it light, making way when another train of tired donkeys lumbered home past them, their brightly coloured tassels swaying on their foreheads.

'Here we are,' he said, stopping at a locked gate on the caldera side of the path. He punched in a number and pushed it open, making way for her.

He saw the surprise on her face when she registered that they were outside a palace, a remnant of the Venetian occupation of Santorini in centuries long past. 'I thought we were going to a restaurant. But this…'

'Is a very private restaurant.'

She turned to him, her blue eyes confused. 'But this is a home. A palace.'

'With the best views in Thera. I'm staying here.'

'*Staying* here? Like a guest?'

He answered with a welcoming sweep of

his arm. 'Come inside, I'll show you the view from the terrace.'

She stayed exactly where she was, half inside the gate and half outside, her head tilted to the side. 'Who are you?'

'I told you. My name is Alexios. Alexios Kyriakos.' He looked at the still-open gate behind her. 'The gate isn't locked from the inside, but I can always leave the gate open, if you prefer, if you think you might need to escape.' He paused for one heavily weighted second. 'If you don't trust me, that is.'

He swore she almost blushed at his mention of trust. Of course, she trusted him now. She shook her head, looking contrite, pushing the loose tendrils of her hair back behind her ears. 'I'm sorry. I'm a little on edge today, especially after what happened at the café. There's no need to leave it open, of course.' And she moved out of the way so he could shut the gate.

He didn't show her inside. Instead he ushered her along a path that wove around the side of the building that opened onto an expansive terrace with a breathtaking view of the islands that made up the broken circle of the caldera, formed in the massive eruption of the volcano beneath thousands of years before. Below them, the almost sheer wall of layered volcanic residue fell away so it felt as if they were suspended over the very edge of the crater. And there, in the gap between the islands, hovered the setting sun, dipping inexorably on its journey towards the sea.

She leaned her hands down on the balustrade, turning her face into the breeze that rushed up the sides of the cliffs, and breathing in the fresh salt air. 'It's magnificent.'

'Isn't it?' He hung back, his hands in his pockets. He didn't crowd her. He didn't hover by her side. He wanted her to feel secure. Safe. It was his pleasure now to watch her. And wait for the right moment.

She turned towards him, the setting sun picking up the golden flecks in her blue eyes, turning them to jewels. Oh, he could wait for the right moment, just so long as he didn't have to wait too long.

'Now,' he said, 'while we wait for the sun to perform its magic, perhaps you would like to eat.' He waved his arm behind, where the doors of the palace had been flung open, to reveal a table set for two dressed in white.

Her brows drew together as she took in the scene. 'How is this possible when we only met this afternoon?'

He smiled, loving her suspicious mind. *If only she knew.* 'The staff were expecting me for dinner,' he said with a shrug. 'I simply called from the café after you agreed to dine with me to ensure there would be enough for two.'

She wandered closer to the table, set with crystal glasses and silverware and tiny vases filled with fresh thyme and rosemary, the scent wafting on the warm breeze like the sheer curtains billowing behind the doorways.

'You understand now why I had no desire to keep this all to myself?'

She nodded. 'It's beautiful. Thank you.'

'Then please sit, and eat, and afterwards we shall enjoy the sunset together.'

As if on cue, the serving staff appeared, delivering warm breads and freshly made dips to the table, followed by pan-fried *saganaki* cheese topped with balsamic figs along with the freshest baby squid, an array of grilled meats and all washed down with the finest Santorini Vinsanto wine.

'It's wonderful,' she said, at one point, leaning back in her chair, her glass of wine in her hand.

He raised his own glass to her. 'It is my pleasure.'

'Tell me,' she asked, leaning forward after

taking a sip of wine, 'why is it that you are here, all alone on Santorini?'

'I am here primarily for business.'

She arched an eyebrow at that, an obvious question. 'Not,' he added, 'that I have a wife or girlfriend I could have brought to accompany me.'

'And why is that?' she asked, gesturing glass in hand to the palace behind and the spectacular caldera view before them. 'When clearly you are a man of means—and, as you are no doubt aware, not entirely unpleasant looks.'

He cocked an eyebrow. '"Not *entirely* unpleasant"? That is good news, indeed. But as to your question, I'm afraid I've been too much of a workaholic. Driven, some might say.'

Especially when it came to the pursuit of justice.

'Although not too driven to chat me up.'

He shrugged. 'Lately I have become aware of how isolated I have become. Meeting you cemented an appreciation of the error of my ways.'

'Wow,' she said, her blue eyes bright. 'That's a heady responsibility you're piling upon my shoulders. I hope you're not going to be disappointed.'

He smiled. 'Now you're laughing at me.'

'I'm sorry. I'm just not used to flirting.'

'Neither am I,' he said with a smile. 'Although I am finding it an entirely pleasurable pastime. If I might be so bold as to ask, why are you here alone?'

'Like I said, Santorini is my favourite Greek island. I like to come here to think.'

'Do you have so much to think about?'

'Who doesn't?' she said with a shrug, not giving anything away. 'What kind of business are you in?'

He smiled at her quick volley, but didn't push it. He'd learned in his dealings with people that the way to make them open up was to pretend indifference, to let them set the agenda. He knew that sooner or later she'd wander back into the topic of her own accord. 'Shipping mainly. Cargo and containers, timetables and paperwork. It's boring.'

'I'm sure it's not,' she said. 'Is it a family business?'

'No. I have no family.'

'What, none at all?'

He gave the briefest shake of his head, feeling a familiar rising tide of bitterness, thinking how different things might have been—*should have been*—if not for the greed and the actions of this woman's father.

He swallowed back on the surge. He didn't need a tidal wave. All he needed now were ripples—a reminder—of why he was here, and why doing this was so right. 'There's nobody,' he said. 'Not now.'

'Oh,' she said, her teeth finding her lip while she blinked too fast. 'It seems we have more than one thing in common. My mother died when I was sixteen. I—I lost my own father a month ago.'

He schooled his features to compassion, even as he smiled inwardly. She might have a sad story, but it was no match for a story of betrayal. 'Is that what you're here on Santorini to think about?'

'Perhaps,' she said, her misty eyes clouding over as she looked away, out towards the sun, now sending a golden-red ribbon of colour across the water. 'Look,' she said, standing. 'The sun is setting.'

He followed her to the balustrade, to where they could see the white buildings that adorned the caldera rim now washed in red, the sun a fat golden orb bending the painted layers of the sky beneath.

'So beautiful,' she said, her eyes fixed on the spectacular display.

She was, he thought, watching her rather than the sunset, and soon she would be his.

The knowledge made him burn. The perfect revenge and the only disappointment was that Stavros wasn't here to see it. But then, it would be a much more extensive—and satisfying—revenge than he'd had planned.

'Look,' he said, putting mere fingertips to the fabric at the small of her back while he pointed out to the midst of the darkening sea, where a sailing boat bobbed in a ribbon of golden light.

'Oh,' she said, and he knew it was because he'd touched her, because he'd felt her shuddering response, and knew she was ripe for the taking.

Oh, yes, he would play this cherished daughter of his nemesis like a fish on a hook. Play her, use her, and then he would break her, just as her father had broken his father.

And then he would walk away.

To Athena, it seemed the sunset was being performed for her and Alexios and for them alone. There was nobody else within earshot, no evidence of other human life beyond a solitary sailing boat far below them on the sea, while the colours around her intensified, the range narrowed to red and gold and every brilliant shade in between.

And then suddenly his hand was gone from

the small of her back, and despite the spectacular glory going on around her it was that tiny touch she missed. Missed his warmth but most of all the spark he'd triggered in her flesh. And now the sun was setting, burning brighter, until it kissed the water and, despite knowing better, Athena held her breath in anticipation of the hiss of steam at the union.

But even the sunset could not make her forget Alexios was still here, close beside her. Never had she been more aware of a man's presence in her life. He was right there at her shoulder. So close she could once again smell the lemon tang of his soap. So close she could feel his body's warmth on her bare arm.

So close.

And yet he didn't make a move towards her.

Slowly, inexorably, the sea embraced the sun, and with every passing second Athena wished he would touch her again, even if only to point out something else.

Though more than that, she wished, leaning closer, her bare arm brushing his, setting her skin alight, that he would kiss her. In this perfect moment with the perfect excuse of the most romantic sunset in the world as a backdrop.

Why did he not try to touch her?

Why didn't he kiss her?

But while the air all but crackled between them, even while her body swayed of its own accord towards his, frustratingly he moved no closer to her. Still, he made no move at all.

By the time the sea swallowed the sun whole and the last glimmer of light was extinguished, her strung-out nerves were at breaking point for fruitless, pointless, wishing.

She reached for and clung to the balustrade with both hands, disappointment weighing heavy in her sigh.

'Amazing,' he said beside her, and his deep voice rippled into the fabric of her soul. She felt silly now that the rush of disappointment was over. All this time she'd been wary and suspicious and all the time he really had only wanted to share a meal and a sunset with someone.

She put her unfamiliar libido back in the dusty box where it had come from. She had no right to be disappointed. She hadn't wanted anything to happen really. It was the sunset and the colour and the heart-stopping beauty of an island the gods had blessed with unimaginable riches to compensate for locating it over an active volcano.

'That was spectacular,' she said, turning her back to the balustrade now the show was over. 'Thank you for sharing it with me, and for a wonderful dinner. I should probably be heading off now.'

'You don't want to stay for coffee?'

She shook her head. She felt foolish now. Carried away by the romance of the island. Reading too much into a simple invitation. If it was any lighter here on the balcony, he would surely see her face glowing red.

She crossed back towards the table where she'd left her bag, searching for a lightness she didn't feel. 'I have a confession to make.'

'You do?'

'I actually thought—I mean—just for a while there, when you took off chasing the thief, well, I'm sorry to admit that I half wondered if you hadn't been working together, and that I'd never see you, or my bag, again.'

He shook his head, his dark eyes glinting with amusement. 'You honestly believed me capable of behaving in such a despicable manner?'

She cast her eyes downwards. 'I'm so sorry. I was strung out. I don't know why else I would have thought such a thing.'

His dark eyes narrowed. His lips turned up on one side. 'But then, you thought I was some kind of gigolo too.'

'God, don't remind me. I'm sorry about that too.'

He leaned an arm up onto the wall beside her and she was struck by the poetry in the slow but sure movement of his muscled limbs. 'You thought I was going to seduce you.'

'To be fair, I didn't know what to think. I was alone and you were very charming. *Are* very charming. What was a woman on her own to think? But you've proved me wrong and I've had the most wonderful evening, thank you.' She put out a hand to shake his.

He stared down at it, a crease tugging dark brows together. 'Are you disappointed?'

'What?'

'That I didn't try to seduce you?'

She shook her head. 'I don't... I'm not sure...'

His eyes met hers, and in their dark depths she saw an insecurity and wavering that mirrored her own, an insecurity she would never have expected to see in this man's, not when he otherwise appeared so confident and assured. An insecurity she instinctively wanted to smooth away and reassure.

'Because you must know,' he said, 'I wanted to kiss you.'

Her mouth went dry. 'You did?'

'When the sun was setting before us and

it was like we were part of it, rather than just watching, and I could see the look of wonder on your face—in that moment I ached to reach out a hand and touch you.'

'You did?' She tossed her head back, trying to inject no more than a casual interest in his revelation. Trying to sound as if they were discussing something academic. 'Why didn't you?'

'Because I was afraid you might run. That it would confirm your worst thoughts about me. So I held back. Let me tell you, removing my hand from your back was one of the hardest things I have ever done.' His dark eyes trained on hers. 'Would you have run?'

Her bag suddenly felt heavy in her hands, her limbs felt boneless and it was all she could do to remember to breathe.

'Would you?'

The air between them seemed to shimmer with expectation. This was no game they were playing. No innocent question and answer session. This felt dangerous.

Reckless.

Athena didn't do reckless.

Not normally. But tonight was far from normal.

And this time that voice inside her head demanded to quash any resistance and to be heard, and this time, she was only too prepared to listen.

'No.' Her answer was a bare whisper, and yet more than a whisper. A confession.

He closed the distance between them and put the pads of his thumb to her cheek, the fingers of his other hand tracing the line of her lips. 'You are more beautiful than any sunset I have ever witnessed. I have wanted you since the moment we first met.'

His warm breath, scented with the cognac they'd shared, caressed her skin, and like the waves upon the sea his words rippled into her soul. Her cheek leaned into his touch, her lips parting, seeking more, tasting him.

'If you ask me to kiss you,' he said, 'there is no way I could refuse.'

Her heart skipped a beat. And she knew with a woman's sense that this was bigger than any kiss. The heat pooling in her belly, the pulse beating at her very core told her this wouldn't stop with a kiss. But he was giving her the choice—stop now or go on.

In the end, it was no choice at all. 'So kiss me,' she said.

And he made a sound, guttural and deep, a sound of triumph mixed with need that rumbled straight to her veins and turned her blood to bubbles as he pulled her close and his lips met hers. Warm lips. Surprisingly soft and yet firm. Engaged in a sensual dance with hers. Slow. Gentle. Teasing. Deeper. *Repeat.*

Her knees turned weak. She reached for him, needing an anchor to steady herself, finding a rock as her hands tangled in the folds of his shirt and found his hard body beneath. Her fingers embraced his sculpted torso and she heard a sound like a whimper and realised it had come from her.

But he was glorious. Muscled and hard beneath her seeking fingers. Thirsty fingers, drinking in the ridges of bone and tight bunches of muscle as his mouth made magic on hers. While his long-fingered hands scooped down the sides of her head, to her shoulders, leaving trails that felt like sparks under her skin and that scorched a path all the way down via peaking nipples, to where an aching heat pulsed between her thighs.

And even as she pressed her body closer to his, closer into his kiss, she knew this was all kinds of reckless, because she knew there was no way this was stopping with a mere kiss.

And she wanted it.

She wanted it all.

CHAPTER FOUR

SO MUCH MORE than a mere kiss! His scent, his taste and the feel of him combined into one powerful cocktail and she wanted more. She parted her lips and he accepted her invitation, his tongue tasting, testing, before engaging hers in a sensual dance of passion and need. She was already lost in sensation, blood fizzing in her veins, when she felt the brush of his thumb against one sensitive nipple, and she gasped into his mouth with the sheer electricity of it.

He growled, liking her response, his hands growing bolder, sweeping from her shoulders to the cheeks of her behind, squeezing, her muscles clenching and tightening in response as his fingertips ventured dangerously close to her cleft.

'*Theos,*' he said, wrenching his mouth from hers. 'Stay, and make love with me, Athena.'

She answered him with her mouth and her

body, pulling his head back to hers, pressing her full length against his body, her plumping breasts hard against his chest, her hips pushed against his. She encountered the evidence of his own arousal and felt a rush of heat hard on the heels of a bloom of delight.

For so long, it seemed, she'd felt numb. Too long. Ever since she'd heard the news of her father's death and been sideswiped by the impact it had on her. By the knowledge that now she had lost both her mother and, even if their relationship had been difficult at times, or maybe because of it, her father.

She'd been operating in a vacuum ever since.

Numb. Emotionless.

But Alexios had awakened something deep inside her and it unfurled and blossomed like a flower that had been buried under a winter snow. It was so good to feel again.

And now, all she wanted to do was feel.

Her feet went from underneath her, as he swept her up into his arms, his lips still on hers. He turned and kicked open a door, before spinning around and kicking it shut behind them. She had an impression of space, of high ceiling and billowing curtains on windows opening to the caldera, before she felt softness at her back as he laid her down in a bed hung with silken drapes of red and gold, the colours of the sunset.

Then he drew back, one knee on the bed, and looked at her in the half-light. 'So beautiful,' he said, and his words gave her hope that her life had turned a corner, and that the bleakness of the last few weeks might be at an end.

He tugged at the buttons on his shirt, pulled it from his shoulders and sent it fluttering to the floor. Her eyes drank him in. Wide shoulders. Sculpted chest and abdomen and arms where muscles rippled with every movement. Arms whose hands were working at his waistband, sliding down the zipper, before they too joined his shirt on the floor.

And all the while, his dark eyes didn't leave hers, their intensity leaving her breathless and giddy, making way for one brief moment of indecision, a sudden bubble of nerves that this was happening too fast. A sudden bubble of rational thought that sprang up unbidden.

As if sensing her momentary panic, he surprised her by reaching down to kiss her again, soothing her, and already it seemed too long that he'd been away, while his hand slid beneath her to ease down the zipper at her back. With every parted tooth she felt her desire intensify and coalesce, until need was at the very essence of her. He was still kissing her as he eased the shoulder straps down her arms, still kissing her as she eased up her hips and let him peel her sundress away, until she was lying on the bed with nothing but a few scraps of lace to shield her from his view, and never, it seemed, had she felt more vulnerable.

Only then did his lips leave hers, leaving her breathless and wanting, as he drew himself back on his heels. 'Magnificent,' he said, and she let go a breath she hadn't realised she'd been holding, before he returned to her, running his strong hands up the outside of her legs, her hips, her waist and shoulders and her breathing ratcheted up another notch as he came closer, scooping her into his arms and rolling her against him.

Skin against skin. His legs tangling with hers, rough versus smooth, corded muscles against toned flesh. His abdomen against hers. Locked from head to toe. An electric connection only heightened by the places still hidden, the places still to be revealed, the places that now ached with potent need.

His hand cupped one breast and she whimpered, arching her back into his touch, while her hands roamed the glory of his sculpted back, muscles shifting with every movement,

fascinating and thrilling her in equal measure, her hands drinking in the perfection of his skin-scape.

And then the lace covering her breasts was gone and she wanted to cry with relief, but when he dipped his head to take one peaked nipple into his mouth, it was a cry of ecstasy she gave as spears of pleasure shot straight to her aching core.

She was already burning up when he turned his attention to her other breast, his seeking hand now free to roam downwards, his fingertips toying with the lace edging of her underwear before inching slowly beneath the lace to cup her mound, before venturing closer to that place where her need pooled and coalesced into a living beast, demanding to be sated. She was breathing hard now, alight with the passion he'd unfurled in her, perspiration beading on her skin as, stoked by his every touch, the flames built up inside.

She was already teetering on the edge, anticipation acting like accelerant on a fire, so when his fingers parted her, finding her slick with want, her nerve endings all but screaming for his touch, she was already primed.

One gliding caress, one gentle pass by no more than a fingertip, and she climaxed against his hand. Hard. The shudders reverberating through her, wave after wave of pleasure rocking her world, until it felt as if he were the only thing anchoring her to the earth.

He kissed her as she came down, raining kisses on her mouth, on her eyes, on her sweat-slickened breasts. 'I'm sorry,' she whispered, suddenly embarrassed and feeling gauche, her inexperience clearly on display.

'Shh…' he soothed. 'Don't be.'

'But…'

'We are just getting started.'

She blinked up at him, still catching her breath, to see him sliding down the band of black underwear at his hips. Her eyes widened in appreciation. Even bigger than she'd imagined when she'd felt the hard press of him against her belly. Even more magnificent. And despite just climaxing, despite thinking she was spent, she felt desire curl upwards inside her like tendrils of fragrance from a scented candle.

He reached across into a drawer beside the bed, ripping open the foil without taking his eyes from hers, rolling the condom down his long length, his eyes daring hers to watch his progress. 'You see what you do to me, *mikro peristeri*? You see how much I burn for you?'

The endearment was sweet, but… 'Why do you call me your little dove?'

'Because since we met,' he said, positioning himself between her legs, leaning on one elbow to slowly sweep the other hand from her hair to her shoulder, over one breast and her belly, and lower, his fingers curving between her thighs, 'you are always on edge. Always looking to fly away.'

She swallowed. It was hard to hold a conversation when a man had his hand—*there*. 'I'm not flying away now.'

'No,' he said with a smile, his fingers traversing her still-sensitive flesh, gently exploring, caressing, circling her tender core. 'You are a gift straight from the gods. How blessed am I that I should have stumbled into your orbit?'

Why he was still trying to pleasure her with his touch and his words, she didn't know. She would enjoy the sex, she had no doubt, but there was no point him wasting his time. She would never climax again, not after having her mind blown so completely and utterly already.

And yet he seemed in no hurry, taking his time, dipping his head again to take each nipple in turn into his hot mouth before returning to her mouth, still intent on pleasuring her. That was when she felt it, felt one long finger slide inside her. Her muscles squeezed in response at the intimate intrusion, and he growled, low in his throat, as he followed it with a second, working in concert with the pad of his thumb, their dance on her tender flesh generating sparks of sensation where she thought there would be none.

But it was impossible.

There was no way.

Except her body had other ideas. Her senses stirred, he seemed to know how much pressure, how much teasing was enough to leave her breathless and wanting more.

And then his fingers slid away, replaced with a new, heated pressure, and for a moment she felt a sense of panic, that perhaps she was being too greedy and wanting it all. 'You are beautiful,' he said, resting on his elbows either side of her, his hands weaving their way into her hair, holding her captive to his kiss.

And as his hot mouth told her that he'd meant what he'd said, she relaxed, her hips angling, tilting to welcome him. He seemed to sense the moment she was ready, for he chose that exact moment to lunge, driving himself deep inside her.

She cried out, not in pain, but in the completion, a delicious feeling of fullness suffusing her flesh while nerve endings lit up like sparks under her skin. And that was before he started to move.

'Oh,' she said, as he slowly withdrew, wanting to cling on, already missing him. But he was back, and then again, slowly accelerating, building the rhythm faster, until their ragged breathing became their accompaniment. And sparks born in the smouldering ruins of her latest climax flared into flame and flickered and danced under her skin, until with one final thrust from Alexios, accompanied by one triumphant cry, her world shook apart again, this time with his name on her lips.

It took longer to find her way back this time, her breathing ragged, her mind blanked from everything but the sudden realisation that all the stuff she'd ever believed about sex and how many times you could achieve orgasm in a night had been incinerated in the heat of their coming together, the ashes scattering to the waters of the bottomless caldera far below.

He stood at the window, looking out over the sleeping crater, a ribbon of silvery light bisecting the inky darkness and lighting a path direct to his room. Lights twinkled on the island across the water, likewise on the yacht, anchored in a bay, while all else was dark.

He looked back at the bed, at the woman lying there in the beam of silver, her hair tangled across her pillow, her lips plump and parted, deeply asleep. She'd fallen into his bed as easily as she'd fallen for his ruse, just as he'd anticipated, but she'd been so much more than he'd expected too. So much more. She'd gone off like fireworks in his bed, responsive, explosive. And then she'd climaxed again, and again, and, by the wondrous look on her face, the last time had surprised her the most.

And he half wished Stavros Nikolides were still alive, so he could witness this moment. So Alexios could bodily drag him in here to see his precious daughter naked and supremely satisfied in the bed of his nemesis, the son of the man he had so badly wronged.

For that would surely kill him all over again.

Moonlight on the blackened caldera waters winked back at him, telling him his logic was flawed. Because if Stavros had been alive, he would have enacted his original plan, and Athena would never have been in his bed, and that would have been a travesty. Revenge this way was so much more satisfying.

There was more than one way for a father to pay, and make him pay he would.

The sins of the father...

He would make Stavros pay dearly.

He curled his hand into a fist, all the injustice he'd felt congealing into concrete within, and thumped it hard against the wall.

She stirred behind him. 'Alexios?' Her voice was husky with sleep. Surprisingly sexy. As she herself had been throughout the night whenever he had reached for her. 'What are you doing? Can't you sleep?'

'I was thinking,' he said.

'About what?'

He flexed his fingers. 'Tomorrow,' he lied. 'I was thinking about what we should do tomorrow.'

'But... Don't you have business to attend to?'

'It can wait.' He paused, arching an eyebrow. 'Unless you don't want to see me again? Are you going to fly away again, *mikro peristeri*?'

She kept him waiting, her teeth troubling her bottom lip, as if weighing it up. Before she said, 'Not if you don't want me to.'

And he smiled as he collected her in his arms and tumbled her back down onto the pillows. 'Perfect.'

* * *

The sails had filled out in the warm breeze, the boat propelled across the bottomless waters of the caldera until they were far away from the newly arrived cruise ships and the well-worn tourist trails. Athena lay on the deck alongside Alexios, content to lie on her back and soak up the sun after a swim in the bottomless waters of the caldera.

From here the walls of the islands rose steeply around them, seemingly insurmountable, the jagged path up the cliff from the port seeming to defy the laws of nature and science. It was different to see the ring of islands that made up the crater's edges from this aspect, the layers of pumice and ash that had spewed more than three thousand years ago from the erupting volcano so clearly visible in the distinctly coloured bands in the cliffs surrounding them.

'What are you staring at?' he asked beside her, rolled onto his side and following her gaze.

She nodded towards the soaring cliffs, thinking of the force of the eruption that had all but resulted in the destruction of the island as it then existed, all but obliterating the civilisation that had once called it home. 'Sorry. I just never cease to be awed by this place. It's hard to believe we're sitting in the middle of a live volcano.'

Especially when the sun turned the surface of the sea to diamonds and the water lapped gently at the sides of the boat. Right now an eruption seemed impossible. Incomprehensible. But there was the evidence, all around them.

'It must have been terrifying when it erupted,' he said. 'I can't imagine what it was like being here.'

'Most people were long gone,' she said, sitting up. 'There were earthquakes, bad ones, over many years. Some people stayed, but many abandoned their homes here and took their families in their ships and fled to Anatolia and to Crete. The lucky ones went early and much further afield.'

'Why lucky?'

'Because it wasn't a simple eruption. That would have been bad enough, but when the sea water rushed into the empty lava chamber, it triggered a tidal wave that travelled for hundreds of miles. The northern coast of Crete, with the fleets of the Minoan traders, they were all destroyed. It wasn't just Santorini, or Thera, as it was known then, that was destroyed. A dark ash cloud encircled the earth, blotting out the sun and wiping out the crops for many years. Even escape to somewhere like Crete proved no escape, just a deferral of the end. It signalled the end of the Minoan civilisation.'

He sat up alongside her, a frown tugging his dark brows together.

'Oh, I'm sorry,' she said, shaking her head. 'In real life I'm an archaeologist and the Minoan civilisation, in particular, is a passion of mine. I studied it at university and I tend to get a bit carried away about it.'

He curled his hand around hers, lifted it to his lips. 'You don't have to be sorry for being passionate. I was never good at history. I was never a good student. Tell me more.'

She smiled, warming to her topic. 'You know some believe the legend of Atlantis started right here, more than three thousand years ago. A fabulously wealthy and cultured civilisation, drowned under the sea and lost for ever.'

He propped himself up on his elbows. 'Do you believe that?'

'I do. It accords with the ancient Egyptian records, and the writings of Plato. The Egyptians traded with the Minoans until their world was suddenly blotted out, and why would that have happened unless some terrible fate had overcome them? Besides,' she added with a smile, 'it makes much more sense than the theory about some mythical island somewhere in the Atlantic that disappeared without trace or explanation, don't you think? Whereas a beautiful island, an advanced civilisation, as good as wiped from the face of the earth—what better candidate than the Minoan civilisation right here in the centre of the then known world?'

He was staring at her face, his dark eyes lit with pleasure and the flames of something much hotter.

'Do you have any idea how animated you look when you talk like this? Your whole face is alight, even the flecks in your eyes sparkle like golden chips in the light.'

She looked down, suddenly embarrassed. 'I warned you. I get a bit carried away.'

His fingers took hold of her chin, turning it back towards him. 'No, don't be embarrassed about being passionate. You make your passion contagious. In fact, I think I know exactly how that volcano felt before it blew.'

And he drew her chin closer at the same time he dipped his head and his mouth met hers.

Something fluttered in her heart as she gave her mouth to his. Something small and indefinable, but like the brush of butterfly wings against her eyelashes. Something insignificant and yet of such import that it seemed her whole world had subtly shifted in a way that had nothing to do with the currents beneath their vessel.

His lips toyed with hers, gentling, caressing, warm breath intermingled, overlaced with the salty scent of the sea, before, slowly, he pulled gently away.

'Happy?' he asked, smiling down at her.

And Athena blinked as she looked into his beautiful face. Not because of his question, but because of the answer bubbling up inside her. Because she was happy, honestly truly happy for the first time in what seemed for ever. Because she felt as if she was truly alive. 'I am.'

'You sound surprised.'

She shrugged. 'Maybe just a little.' She gave a blissful sigh. It was the island, she told herself, for Santorini had once again proved to be her refuge and her saviour. There was a reason she loved this place.

His hand took hers and she felt that zing of excitement, that thrill of connection, she felt every time he touched her, before he lifted it to his lips, and turned it and kissed her palm, his hot tongue stroking it, his dark eyes filled with the promise of dark deeds, sending a delicious thrill coursing through her.

'I like your bikini,' he said, his eyes scanning the length of her body without his head shifting, his voice low and thick and vibrating with so much desire it was impossible not to feel aroused. 'I'm going to enjoy peeling it off.'

Her nipples peaked and hardened as his eyes lingered at her breasts even while his fingers toyed with the tie at her hips, the electric touch of his fingertips setting sparks beneath her skin while his lips came down to meet hers, their heat enough to melt any thought of resistance away. The white bikini had been an impulse decision when he'd suggested sailing today and she'd told him she hadn't brought a swimsuit. A good one as it turned out. He'd taken her to a boutique and she'd been rifling through the racks of one-pieces when he'd offered her a clutch of bikinis. She'd almost said no outright—she hadn't worn a two-piece since she'd been that cock-sure teen A-lister baring almost everything she had to bare on the Amalfi Coast—but something in his eyes had made her reconsider and agree to try them on.

And that very first one, the white one—she'd seen the heat and hunger as his eyes had roamed her exposed flesh, a hunger that had made her insides tremble with the promise of the forbidden. Not some spoilt son of a newspaper tycoon or shipping magnate looking at her with an overactive libido and clumsy technique, but a man, looking at a woman, and wanting her.

As he wanted her now.

He broke away from the kiss, the curled hairs of his sun-warmed chest kissing her bare skin as it rose and fell with his ragged breathing. 'We should take this downstairs,' he said, his heated breath on her face, like an invitation. And in the flutter of her answering heart, she knew it wasn't just the island that made her so happy. It was this man beside her and the way he made her feel. As if she was special.

As if she deserved to be happy.

And after the despair of the last few weeks, of the shock of learning her estranged father had died, and the remorse she felt for a relationship gone badly wrong, and then the guilt on learning he'd forgiven her without ever letting her know, this man made her feel things might have changed, that her life was on the up.

She went willingly as he tugged her to her feet. Went willingly down through the hatch to the freshly made bed in the spacious cabin lined with glossy timbers with brass fittings. And here he finished what he'd started, tugging at the tie between her breasts, brushing the thin straps over her shoulders and letting her bikini top fall to the floor, before his hands moved to her thighs, untying the bows at her sides until that scrap of material similarly fell to the floor.

He didn't reach for her straight away. His eyes drank her in and, while she stood naked before him, she saw the movement in his throat as he swallowed, and witnessed the smouldering heat of his eyes.

Emboldened by the memory of a night of carnal pleasure reinforced by what she saw in his features, she reached for him, one hand cupping his length through his swimming shorts, the other sliding beneath the band at his hips so he was encircled by her fingers from in front and behind.

Breath hissed through his teeth as his head fell back. *'Theos!'* he uttered. 'What you do to me, Athena.' Before his hands found her waist and he half lifted, half tossed her to the bed, his black bathers swept down his legs before he joined her.

'What do I do?' she asked, liking this new power she now had, and half intoxicated herself at the feel and sight of him, rigid and bucking and wanting her.

He growled, pinning her arms beside her head as he positioned himself between her legs. 'You make me want to do this...'

She had no time to react. No time to pay heed to that niggling thought in the back of her head. No time before she felt him, easing into her heated body.

And then there was no time for anything but the sheer joy of their coupling as he filled her. Sensation radiated through her, wiping thought and logic and any hint of rationality away. While the boat rocked, the deep blue waters of the caldera slapping at the windows, accompanied by the rhythmic sounds of their lovemaking.

Her last and only thought as they tumbled together over the edge again was that a girl could get used to this.

His harsh curse brought her out of her post-coital bliss. 'What is it?'

He pulled away roughly. 'I'm sorry, I didn't use a condom. Are you safe?'

Athena blinked. If he only knew. She hadn't had sex with anyone for years. 'Yes.'

He groaned a sigh of relief, relaxing back onto the bed and pulling her close, spooning his body against hers. 'You see what you do to me?' He pressed his lips to her shoulder. 'Thank God one of us was thinking about protection.'

Oh, she thought, *that* kind of safe. Surely, there was no chance. Her cycle had never been regular, but still it had to be too early…

And she could hardly go back on what she'd said now. He'd made her feel desirable, even wanton, and she didn't want to admit the truth and sound naïve and unsophisticated. She was twenty-seven, of course he'd assume she'd take precautions. So instead she picked up his hand from where it was wrapped around her breasts, and lifted it to her mouth. 'Thank God,' she said, sending a little prayer that she was right as he snuggled her closer and pressed his mouth to that sensitive place where her shoulder met her throat, making her mewl, and pushing any hint of concern to the back of her mind.

It was almost too easy. Alexios gazed down at her, stretched out on the deck with her head resting on her folded arms and looking boneless and utterly spent. The sun was sinking lower in the sky and soon the boat would come to ferry them back to the shore, and to the Venetian palace at Thera where Alexios had invited her once again for dinner.

This time she hadn't hesitated, but then, he hadn't expected her to. In no time he'd bent her to his will and she was as good as his. Soon he would give the signal to Anton to prepare the paperwork that would hand her father's precious fortune to him.

So much easier than dealing with her father. So much more satisfying.

She looked so innocent lying there. So sweet and so blissfully unaware of what he had planned.

He sighed, admiring the way the white bikini showed off her curves, leaving her slim waist on show; remembering the look on her face when she'd climaxed—her body hitched, her blue eyes open wide and almost shocked, her lush mouth halted, mid gasp. And then her head had been flung back as she'd exploded around him.

It was almost a shame it had to end.

The noise of a motorboat cut through his thoughts. The boat he'd summoned to take them back to the shore. She stirred at the approaching sound, rolling over and stretching out long arms like a cat rising from slumber. 'Is that our boat?' Even her sleepy voice sounded like a purr.

He knelt down. 'I'm afraid it's time to go, *mikro peristeri.*'

She smiled up at him, snaking an arm around his neck and pulling his lips towards hers. 'I've had the best day, Alexios. Thank you.'

'I'm glad,' he said, as he smiled into her kiss. But why wouldn't he smile? Because whoever said revenge was a dish best served cold hadn't been doing it right.

Revenge served hot, with an all too willing participant like Athena, was revenge worth taking.

He felt the warmth of her sun-kissed skin against him, he tasted the sultry heat of her mouth, and he felt himself grow hard.

This was right.

This was the very best kind of revenge.

CHAPTER FIVE

ATHENA LAY IN Alexios's big bed, sleep evading her. By rights, she figured, after a day out on the caldera alternately swimming and making love, she should be sleeping like a log. But she'd dozed on and off throughout the day, snug and content, and she was too wound up to sleep.

She looked sideways, at the dark silhouette of the man sleeping beside her, his arm still looped lazily behind her neck, his fingers draped over her shoulder, still holding her close even in sleep.

She nestled her head back into the crook of his shoulder on a sigh. Was it only yesterday that they'd met?

It hardly seemed possible to feel so comfortable with anyone so quickly, not when she was usually so guarded, and yet it had been so easy with this man. He seemed to have a way of getting under her defences and break-

ing down her barriers. She couldn't remember the last time she'd spent two consecutive nights in a man's bed. Now it seemed hard to imagine sleeping by herself, going to sleep without strong arms around her, waking up alone. It occurred to her that she would miss it.

Inside her chest, she felt that flutter of butterfly wings sensation again, except this time it was enough to make her breath jag.

What was happening to her? For years she'd survived—even prospered—without a man in her life. No doubt she would again.

And for all his assurances, telling her there was no woman in his life because he was driven and a workaholic, it was hard to believe he'd spent the last however many years living like a priest. He was too good-looking. Too charming. And in bed, way too much a man to have spent all his days and nights alone.

Which made her wonder—was this just one more in a long string of temporary affairs to him? Despite Alexios's protestations, did he make a habit out of picking up random women wherever he happened to be situated, flattering them all the same way? Bedding them all the same way?

She swallowed down on the bubble of disappointment that accompanied that question. She had no right to be disappointed. He was nothing to her. She was nothing to him. Still, in spite of her doubts and unanswered questions, she wasn't ready for this to end just yet, whatever 'this' turned out to be. Even if this was only ever destined to be a brief affair.

And if she was going to be realistic, what else could it be? Soon she would have to return to her life and her work at the Department of Antiquities. But for now, she thought, her eyelids finally feeling heavy, she would enjoy being treated as if she was special. As if she was cherished.

As Alexios made her feel.

She snuggled under the arm that encircled her shoulders, relishing the tang of his scent around her, salty and masculine, her body tingling at the memories invoked by the musky scent of sex. She sighed against him as her body relaxed against his. Might as well enjoy these days and nights while they lasted.

Slow and gentle. Sweeping and smooth. She awoke to sensation, to rhythm, to the feel of fingers against skin as his hand skimmed the curves of her body—knee to thigh, thigh to hip, and over, to that curve to waist and up her rib cage, to squeeze, tantalisingly close

to her breasts before starting the slow slide down her body again.

Her breath caught, moving from sleep to wakefulness in sheer moments, everywhere his fingers touched suddenly alight, electric, and sparking with increasing desire with each sweeping stroke of his hands.

She stirred, purring, turning to be closer to him, to be able to reach for him and snuggle against his warm body.

He pressed his lips to her throat. 'Did I wake you?'

She made a sound like a purr. 'Mmm... Yes.'

'I'm sorry,' he said, his breath a warm whisper on her skin as he kissed his way across the curve of her shoulder, and lower, his lips pausing to capture one tight nipple.

'Don't be,' she said, her body sparking into wakefulness now, before his mouth moved still further south, her belly tightening on a gasp at the brush of his whiskered jaw and the sudden realisation of where he was heading.

And as he parted her legs and dipped his head between, the flick of his tongue assaulting her senses, she remembered the thoughts she'd had when finally her body had surrendered to sleep. Who cared if this was permanent or not? There were worse things in life than having a fling with a man who made you feel as if you were the centre of his existence, even if it did only last for a few short days and nights.

She woke to the sound of her phone, and blinked, confused, into wakefulness. She was alone, the sheets alongside her cool, and she vaguely remembered Alexios kissing her, and promising he would see her later, after some meeting he had.

She yawned as she retrieved her phone, smiling when she saw who the caller was. 'Professor, how are you?'

'Where are you?' her old friend and mentor said, sounding agitated. 'I went to your apartment but there was no answer.'

'I'm in Santorini,' she said. 'What's wrong?'

'Nothing's wrong,' he said. 'It's a ship. Divers have found the wreck of a Minoan ship loaded with ingots off the coast of Cyprus— and, Athena, even under the scum of millennia, the ingots have a gold-red glow…'

Sensation spider-webbed through her, an electric network that left her tingling from her head down to her toes.

Orichalcum.

The fabled reddish-gold metal of Atlantis, long thought a myth, until a few years ago,

when a wreck had been found off the coast of Sicily. And Athena realised it wasn't agitation she was hearing in his voice, it was excitement, the same excitement she now felt fizzing in her blood. A Minoan ship that would have sailed the length of the Mediterranean and beyond. A ship that would have sailed in the waters of Santorini as it was then, a wealthy and highly civilised hub of the Minoan trading world.

'How many people know about this?'

'Not many. A few fishermen.'

'The site needs to be secured,' she said, recalling the trouble the authorities had had with looting with the shipwreck found in Sicilian waters, and already out of bed and sorting through her clothes. 'How soon can we mount an expedition?'

The professor tut-tutted at the end of the line. 'That might not be as easy as we might wish for. I've approached the minister for funding, but it's difficult—the department has been asked to cut back. The entire government has. To make an exception for one project…'

'But they have to fund this! This is Hellenic Bronze Age heritage. If what you're saying is right, this will be ten times more significant than the Sicilian discovery.'

'I know,' he said. 'It's potentially the most significant discovery of its kind and this time in Greek waters. I don't know what they're thinking.' Athena could almost see Loukas scratching his wispy grey-haired head in despair. She understood that the government was cash-strapped and needed to prune back spending, but it was ridiculous to delay and risk letting a find like this slip through their fingers, as it would if an immediate expedition couldn't be financed. Word would spread, the looters and souvenir seekers would move in, and soon there would be nothing left to discover, and an opportunity to learn more about the Minoan civilisation would go begging. There had to be some way.

It hit her then, the fact that she was no longer a poor archaeologist, having to wait upon the success of grant applications and the largesse of benefactors.

She crossed back to her bag, dug out the card the lawyers had given her, along with an undertaking to help her at any time. They could start by helping her now.

'Forget the ministry, we'll do it ourselves. Make some calls, Loukas, and see if you can get a couple of boats and a team together. I'll be on the next flight back to Athens.'

'But how? Some will volunteer their time,

but how are we going to find the kind of boats we need without funding?'

'I'll fund it.'

'You?'

Athena smiled, thinking she might as well take advantage of this new mad world she had found herself in. 'This might come as a bit of a shock, Loukas, because it sure did for me, but as of two days ago, it seems I'm a billionaire.'

Anton was waiting in his office when Alexios got there, one eyebrow arched at his late arrival for their morning appointment. '*Yassou*, Anton,' Alexios said as he sat down at his desk, ignoring the sly question in his offsider's eyes. It was none of his employee's business why he'd kept the man waiting.

'Everything is ready,' Anton said. 'As soon as you give the word, I will organise the paperwork transferring the girl's shareholding in the Nikolides empire to you. The collapse of the Nikolides empire. First the property portfolio, then the shipping business, and finally, Argos island itself. All of it, delivered neatly into your lap.'

'Good man,' Alexios said, only half listening, glancing over the business emails that required his attention this morning.

'Well?' the other man pressed. 'When do you want me to start the fireworks?'

'I'll let you know. Thank you, Anton.'

But the other man clearly wasn't about to be dismissed. He leaned down, the knuckles of his fisted hands resting on the desk. 'I thought you wanted this. I thought you wanted to avenge the wrongs after what Stavros did to your father.'

The hackles on the back of Alexios's neck rose. 'Did I ever say that I didn't? There is no need to remind me of the plans I have been working towards for ten years. I'll decide when the time is right. And I promise you, you'll be the first to hear.'

His offsider bent his elbows before pushing himself from the desk, his mouth tight, his movements rigid and stiff. He looked like a man fighting himself.

'Is there a problem, Anton?'

'No, no problem.' He spat out the words like bullets, the untruth he'd spoken crystal clear to see. 'I just don't know why you would want to wait.'

'Why are you so worried? Is the plan at risk of being discovered if we have to wait one or two more days?'

'Well, no.'

'Then I will do it in my time, Anton. Not

yours. Athena is hardly going to sign a stack of papers shoved under her nose without a good reason. I'm in the process of finding that good reason.'

The other man exhaled on a sigh, adding a curve to his lips that barely passed as a smile. 'Of course. I have just worked so hard for this. To get this far...'

Alexios rose to his feet, sick of being spoken down to. '*We* have all worked so hard for this, no one more so than me. Which is why I intend enjoying every minute of it. The woman is almost exactly where I want her. The more she trusts me, the harder this will hit her. Don't you agree?'

Anton nodded even as a tic plucked at his cheek. 'Of course. Let me know. I'm ready when you are.'

'Excellent,' Alexios said, rounding his desk. 'I will let you know when I am.' He slapped his colleague on the back. 'Thank you, Anton.'

This time the man took his cue. He nodded, briefly, before letting himself out.

Alexios sighed. If there'd been prizes for rat cunning at the Kostas Foundation School, Anton would have scooped the pool, but there were still lessons the former street kid had to learn. It was one thing to be keen to carry out your boss's plans, it was another thing entirely to adopt them as your own.

Yes, Alexios would exact his revenge, nothing surer, but there was no desperate rush, not when the silken web he was building around her grew ever tighter. Whenever he gave the word, and only when he gave the word, the axe would fall. And the more Stavros's daughter trusted him, the more it would blindside her.

The more it would destroy her.

And the more complete would be his revenge.

Meanwhile, the more time he would have to enjoy her.

The housekeeper reluctantly gave her directions to Alexios's office, but only after Athena told her it was urgent that she see him. Even if this was just a short fling to him, she still owed him an explanation as to why she was leaving in such a hurry. She smiled as she hurried down the stairs, remembering his term of endearment for her and why he had called her that. She wasn't his little dove, not really, just as she wasn't fleeing, so much as making a tactical withdrawal.

Already she could see the sense in going back to work. This place and this man had woven some kind of magic spell around her. Santorini had always been able to do that. Alexios just added another layer to the spell.

Away from Santorini—away from Alexios—she could probably put what had happened the last couple of days into some sort of perspective. Back in her real life, whether in her shabby office in the concrete building that housed the Department of Antiquities, or out at sea, on an expedition that promised to provide more clues into the world of the ancients, this would all seem just a dream.

And Alexios had had his fun. Better for her to leave now than for him to tire of her and ask her to leave. At least she could leave with her ego intact.

She rounded the last corner as someone emerged through a door she knew from the housekeeper's directions must lead into Alexios's office. Backlit by bright sunshine from the room, for a second she almost thought it must be Alexios, until the man simultaneously lifted his hand and dipped his head—almost like a bow—before brushing roughly past her in the passageway.

'*Signomi,*' she said pointedly, thinking he was the one who should apologise, but there was no response, just the staccato slap of his shoes climbing the marble of the stairs behind her.

So be it. At least it meant the meeting was over and Alexios was free. She rapped on the door, heard a stern, 'What is it now?' and tentatively opened the door.

'I'm sorry, I needed to see you.'

He looked up from behind his desk, immediately on his feet and crossing the floor to her. 'Oh, it's you.' He lifted a hand to her neck, sliding it under the messy knot of hair she'd tied at the back of her head, and it was impossible not to lean into the warm stroke of his fingers. 'I thought it was somebody else.'

She glanced over her shoulder. 'You mean the man who just left? He didn't seem very happy.'

His fingers stalled. His brows drew closer together, in his eyes a flash of concern. 'You spoke to him?'

She shook her head. 'Not really, he just wasn't very polite. Anyway, that's not why I'm here.'

'Of course not,' he agreed, relaxing a little, taking her by the hand and leading her to the windows opening to the caldera, where the warm salt air swirled and danced in the curtains and played with the ends of her hair.

He leaned back against the door frame and turned her to face him, one hand smoothing the wayward tendrils of her hair. He smiled as the breeze promptly undid his good work. 'But you are, so tell me what is so important that you need to tell me?'

His touch was warm where his fingers grazed her cheek, his breath tinged with coffee that she would taste if only she touched her lips to his, and it occurred to her again that she would miss this—that she would miss him. 'I'm leaving, Alexios. I need to return to Athens immediately.'

'No.' His fingers froze, his frown returning. 'That's not possible.'

She laughed a little. His tone was suddenly hard, his words emphatic. In her wildest dreams she'd been hoping for disappointment rather than relief, but he sounded as if he was almost annoyed at her news. 'I'm sorry, but I have no choice. I have to go.'

'But why? You told me you had time off. Why do you have to leave now?'

She drew back, puzzled. He really was angry. 'I do. But that doesn't mean I can stay here for ever. I have my work. You have yours. And I think both of us knew this was bound to end some time.'

'That doesn't mean it has to end now!' He

rose to his feet, his back to her at the window, one hand raking through his dark hair.

'Why are you so angry?'

He sighed, the tight-bunched shoulders visibly relaxing before he turned. 'I'm sorry,' he said with a smile. 'My meeting could have gone better and then you took me by surprise. But tell me, what is so urgent that you have to leave? Would it help if I told you I wanted you? I didn't want you to go?'

She smiled. Of course, it helped, but her ego more than anything. 'I'd love to stay longer, but I have no choice. There's been a discovery, the remains of a shipwreck, more than three thousand years old. It was carrying orichalcum—do you know how special that is? There's only been one other ship found with such a cargo, and that was in Italian waters and nowhere near as ancient. This is a huge find. There are teams to be put together and expeditions to be arranged.'

'And there is nobody else who can arrange these things?'

'I'm sorry, Alexios,' she said, cupping his jaw with her hand, gratified because he seemed genuinely disappointed and she was eager for him to understand. 'This is my area of speciality. A find like this—it's what every archaeologist dreams about their entire life. I'm not missing out on this.'

'How long will it take?'

'I don't know. It depends on how soon we can make the arrangements. Summertime is best for diving, and already—' She shrugged, looking out on the picture-perfect September day. 'It won't stay like this for long. We can't delay.'

'Then you won't miss out. I'll take you.'

She thought of her tiny apartment handy to the university but in a suburb Alexios would probably never have set foot in. 'There's no need.'

'I'm not losing you, Athena,' he said, taking her hands in his, squeezing them gently. 'Not now, not after taking so long to find you.'

This time it was an entire swarm of butterflies that took off in Athena's belly, their fluttering wings a cloud rising so high she had to swallow to prevent them escaping. She was so unprepared for this. She'd expected a few words of feigned regret, she'd expected a measure of relief from him that it was over, that it wasn't him who had to break the bad news. Not once had she anticipated that he might want whatever was happening between them to be any more than a quick fling. 'In that case, I expect I'll be in Athens when I'm not on site. There's no reason we can't meet up again, if that's what you want.'

'You know I do,' he said, pulling her closer to his mouth. 'You don't get away from me that easily, *mikro peristeri.*'

Athena melted into his kiss, the heart inside her chest feeling warm and wanted, knowing it wasn't goodbye, knowing it wasn't the end, but that maybe, after the turmoil and grief of the last few months, her life was taking a new, happier path. A Minoan shipwreck to explore to fill her days, and this man, to share her nights. Could life get any better?

'Go and pack your things and I will organise the helicopter.'

'Oh, I've already booked a flight…'

'Flights are for ordinary people, Athena. You are not ordinary. You are a very special woman. You fly with me.'

And the way he pulled her closer and kissed her made her want to believe him.

He stood at the windows, staring out over the island-ringed sea, watching but unseeing what was happening below on the sea, while she packed her belongings.

Her leaving was never part of his plans, at least not until he pulled her world apart and she fled, as destitute and broken as his father was.

But then, not even he, who had waited so long for revenge, could have planned for this eventuality. A shipwreck that dated back to the very period she specialised in—what were the chances?

But revenge wouldn't wait. He wasn't about to let her go when he was so close. His plan had changed direction once before. It could do so again. It would make no difference to the result.

Far below, a tender negotiated its way along the dock, disgorging its cargo of tourists wearing baseball caps and straw hats and who gazed agog up the steep steps that led to the town high above.

Like he suddenly was, changing his focus, because there was an upside in this latest development too.

And maybe it was better that when her world suddenly unravelled she'd be far away from here? Then he could simply walk away, leaving her to lick her wounds alone, the price she would pay for the sins committed by her father.

He shook his head. Her father really should have been a better man, and not left his daughter so exposed. It was almost a shame.

Almost.

A car whisked them to the airport and the waiting helicopter, for the short flight to Athens, where another car was waiting to take Athena to her home.

'I'd better give you my address,' she said, as Alexios handed her into the car.

He didn't waste his time listening while she gave the driver the details.

He didn't need to.

He had a file on all things Athena.

He already knew where she lived.

Athena was still glowing when the car pulled up outside her apartment, still on an endorphin high that had started with the fabulous news of the shipwreck, and ended with Alexios insisting on not only accompanying her back to Athens, but doing it in style in his own helicopter. And there was no hint of her good mood letting up any time soon. Not with this man in her life.

'I'll see you to the door,' he said, handing her out, and to Athena it seemed that endorphins bounced and sparkled in the air between them. Something pinged in her heart then, and her breath hitched, so she felt light-headed and hyperaware. The warmth of his hand around hers. The brush of their linked

hands against her hip. The shift in the air as it made way for them.

Was this how falling in love felt, she wondered, as if the whole world was alive and alight with colour and joy? Could it be possible that she was falling in love with Alexios?

He gathered her under his arm, and there was no time to wonder at her discovery, no time to pull it apart, and examine it, only to marvel that fitting in with his body seemed the most natural thing in the world, as if their bodies were made to go together. She snuggled her face against his shoulder, drinking in his sandalwood-spiced aftershave blended with the beguiling scent of man.

'You smell delicious,' she said as they reached the front door.

'And you,' he said, turning her back to the door, 'taste delicious.' He kissed her then, sandwiched between his hard body and the door, his lips and tongue and hot mouth combining to send her bones to jelly and her senses into disarray, right there at the front door of her apartment block.

It must be love, she guessed, as he broke the kiss, his nose resting against hers, their ragged breath intermingling. Otherwise why would her heart be tripping so crazily and her blood all but fizzing in her veins? And why would she feel such a powerful connection that her body was drawn magnetically to be with his?

'Maybe,' he said, his warm breath like a magical potion that made her want more, 'we should take this upstairs.'

She curled her arms around his neck and pressed herself tighter to him, because she didn't want this day to end either. 'I like the way you think.'

He dismissed his driver and together they tumbled into her bed. In the grips of her passion, she didn't care that her apartment was in the dodgy end of Athens and that it was small and modest compared to the spacious palace they'd left behind in Santorini. She didn't care that her furniture was second hand and worn or that Alexios might think less of her now he'd seen where she lived. All she cared about was that Alexios was in her bed, his scent on her pillows and his limbs tangled with hers.

Dawn cast a soft light through the curtains. Athena winced, not at the dark silhouette of the man sleeping beside her, but at what it revealed. For the light might be flattering, but still it couldn't disguise how modest her tiny

apartment really was. Alexios must be thinking he was slumming it.

She had to get up for work soon, the excitement of the shipwreck would see her at work early to start planning the recovery expedition, but suddenly it seemed important to come clean. She trusted him after all. Last night she'd half convinced herself she loved him.

Beside her, he stirred, stretching, his arm seeking her. Finding her and curling around to draw her close to his body and his whiskered cheek. '*Kalimera*, Athena,' he said, his voice as gravelly as his cheeks, before he kissed her, shifting his body so his morning erection pressed hard against her thigh as he kissed his way down her throat. Her heart did that fluttering thing again and Athena suspected she was right. She'd had boyfriends before, when sex was all there was to tie her to them. She knew all about how lust felt. This was different. More special. Deeper.

'I have to go to work,' she protested, squirming, battling her own desires as much as his advances.

'Later,' he murmured, his mouth busy nuzzling her skin, his wonderful big hands roaming her body, drinking in her softness.

'No.' She put her hands over his. 'I'm serious, Alexios. There's something I need to tell you. It's important.'

His body stilled. He drew his head back from where his mouth had been. 'Oh? Like what?'

She smiled, wondering if he thought she was going to tell him she loved him. Wasn't that the kind of thing that struck fear into the hearts of men everywhere, especially when they imagined they were simply having a fling? But even if she suspected it might be the truth, it was too soon to put it into words. They were too new, these feelings unfurling in her chest; too fragile to reveal just yet. She had to be sure, of herself before she could admit it—and sure of him.

She took a deep breath, smiling at the crease in between his eyebrows. 'It's not bad, I promise. It's just—well, I know you must be wealthy. Nobody has a helicopter and drivers at their beck and call if they're not.'

'My business is successful,' he conceded, 'that's true.'

'And I know you think I'm just a poor archaeologist, and really, I am—or I was—but I came into an inheritance recently. It seems, when my father died a few months back, he left me a bit of money.'

Alexios let her go and raised himself up on one elbow, and she gazed up at him in the half-light. He was beautiful in the mornings, his thick hair all designer bedhead and deliciously so, his jaw and cheeks lined with stubble. He reached a hand up to rub that jawline now, and she could almost feel the delicious abrasiveness of his whiskers against her own fingertips. 'A bit?'

'Well, more than a bit, really. More like a lot. My father was Stavros Nikolides. Have you heard of him?'

Alexios blinked hard, pinching the top of his nose between his fingers, trying to swallow against the bile that rose in his throat at the mention of that name before it could leach in and poison his words. How could he tell her that her father was the reason he was here in her bed? 'There are not many in Greece who would not have heard of that man.'

She nodded, accepting his words as the truth, clearly reading nothing more into his flat delivery. 'He left everything to me. His businesses. His fortune. Everything.'

He scanned her face. 'How do you feel about that?'

She shrugged. 'Weird. It's still hard to believe. I'd only found out that day in Santorini that we met. Remember you said I looked like I had the weight of the world on my shoulders?'

He remembered. He remembered the little-girl-lost expression on her face as she'd stared into space. He remembered the feeling that had fuelled him that day, that he was so close to realising his dream, he could taste it. He felt the memory of that feeling twist and squirm in his gut, a living thing, a serpent, promised a meal and gone unfed. Hungry.

Soon, he told it, trying to quieten the writhing beast so that he might talk without it twisting its way out of his mouth. 'I remember.' The two words came out with a gravel crust.

She didn't notice the trouble he was having. It was as if she was focused on the past, her mind full of remembering that day and the feelings it invoked, just as he was. 'I felt like I was being crushed under the news. It was so unexpected—too much to take in. I was shocked, and I was sad too, because I never knew what he'd done and I never had a chance to even say goodbye.'

He growled and pushed himself up higher in the bed. He didn't want to hear about her regrets. He had no regrets about his plans, not

when it came to Stavros Nikolides. 'So you're
no longer just a poor archaeologist?'

'Not any more.' She smiled. 'I hope you
don't mind I didn't tell you before.'

'I thought you trusted me.'

'I do! You showed me I could trust you
from the first day we met. It's just taken a lot
to come to terms with. You do understand,
don't you, why I couldn't tell you? I had to
be—cautious.'

'I understand. Thank you for trusting me
enough to tell me.' He curled an arm around
her shoulders to pull her close for his kiss.
'Maybe it is time I made my own confession.'

She drew back. 'What confession?'

'The palace in Santorini. I wasn't just a
guest.'

Her head tilted, her eyes narrowed. 'It's
yours?'

'It's mine.'

'Wow.' She smiled, one eyebrow cocked.
'If I'd realised I was being picked up by such
a well-heeled gigolo, I might have agreed to
have dinner with you earlier.' She was teasing now, her fingernails raking lazy circles
around his nipples.

He snatched her hand in his, the danger
passed. He'd been right to change the direc-

tion of the conversation, but it wasn't just that, he knew. Because she had a way of unravelling the knotted serpent in his gut, of placating it. Because of course he hadn't forgotten his dream. She was eating out of his hand, wasn't she? She was opening up to him and telling her her secrets—just as he'd planned for her to do. 'I thought that if you knew it was mine, it might scare you off.'

She conceded a laugh. 'You're probably right. I was already on edge that day.' Her eyes narrowed, she smiled up at him. 'So... just how much are you worth?'

'A few billion.' He shrugged. 'The exact number's not important to me.'

'What is important?'

Honouring my deathbed promise to my father.

'What I can do with it. Grow something to ensure the future security of my family and my employees.'

Not to mention, fund my revenge...

'But you don't have a family.'

'I will, one day.' *When the serpent in his gut had been satisfied and he could move on.* 'When I find the right woman.'

After all, his parents had been happily married for the best part of forty years before the balance of their years was cruelly stolen from them. He knew such things were possible. He'd just been too focused to bother with anything but the most physical of relationships until he'd made good on his deathbed promise to his father. Meanwhile it didn't hurt his case one bit to see a blush creeping up Athena's cheeks, and he could tell she was wondering whether she might be the one.

Not a chance.

'Anyway, does that change anything, that we both have money?'

She shook her head. 'No, not at all. It's kind of funny, when you think about it. I mean, what are the chances of running into another billionaire when you sit down at a café for coffee?'

He gave a wry smile, tucking loose tendrils of her hair behind her ear, and kissed the tip of her nose, knowing that chance had nothing to do with it. 'It seems the goddess of wisdom and the defender of mankind have something else in common.'

'And that's good, isn't it?'

'How do you mean?'

'Because everyone warned me to watch out for gold-diggers who might want to help relieve me of my fortune. But if you've got your own money, you're hardly going to come after mine.'

His chin lifted, he kind of smiled as the arm around her shoulders tightened. 'Why would I want to do that?' he said, even as the serpent writhed and convulsed and grew long, sharp spines that lodged deep, deep down in his gut.

CHAPTER SIX

ATHENA SAT ALONGSIDE Loukas in his office, going over the plans for the expeditions. Dust motes danced on what sunlight managed to make it through the grimy office windows, before the dull rays illuminated the bookshelves that lined the walls, and the papers littering his ancient desk. In the midst of a room that looked as well used as Loukas, Athena's laptop was the only concession to modern times.

Divers, dinghies, sonar equipment and security, Athena made sure they covered every contingency. And if she could have paid to guarantee calm weather, she would have done that too.

Loukas looked up when they had finished, satisfied that the expedition could get underway as soon as they could secure the necessary boats. 'This is a wonderful thing for you to do, Athena, to use your own money in this way.'

'To tell you the truth, I was embarrassed when the lawyers told me how much I was worth. And seriously, what else would I do with it? There's far too much for one person and it's nice to be able to do something useful with it.'

Loukas grunted his assent. 'And all this time you had no idea your father had named you as beneficiary?'

'The last I knew was the letter that came from his lawyers years ago, telling me I'd been disinherited. I have no idea when he changed his mind, or why. Perhaps because I was his only child and there was nobody else?' She shrugged.

'Perhaps,' Loukas conceded. 'But maybe too because he was proud of you, and the way you excelled at your studies and with the work you are doing.'

Was it possible her father was proud of her? Athena thought back to the rare meetings they'd had, usually over lunch or dinner at one of Stavros's favourite restaurants. He'd ask her about her studies and her work, but she'd always got the impression he'd simply been trying to make conversation with a daughter he'd barely known after being estranged for years. 'He never told me that.'

'Was he the kind of man to wear his emotions on his sleeve?'

She laughed a little, remembering back to the yelling matches that had followed her out of whichever of his mansions she'd happened to be staying in. 'Hardly, though he had no problems showing his disapproval when he was angry. Though admittedly that was in my rebellious teenage years. I don't think I gave him too much to be proud of back then. It wasn't really a surprise when he disinherited me. Though it cost me.'

'Because you had to fend for yourself?'

'Some, but mostly it cost me in friends. Somehow I wasn't the popular party girl any more. One by one they drifted away.'

Her phone beeped and she reached for it. Alexios, of course, who was already making plans for dinner tonight, a different restaurant every night, a different view of coastline or harbour, and afterwards, lovemaking long into the night. She smiled, her inner muscles already tingling in anticipation. The man was insatiable.

Loukas was watching her when she put her phone down, the eyes in his creased face narrow and sparking with curiosity. 'Is something happening, Athena?'

'What do you mean?'

'You seem different. Happier.'

'How can I not be happy when we're about to embark on an expedition of a lifetime?'

'Yes, this is true, and yet, are you sure that's all it is? You're paying a lot more attention to your phone than you usually do. Are you sure you haven't found a new friend?'

She was about to deny it. It was too early and too new, and who knew where what was happening between her and Alexios would end up and when? But this was her mentor, her oldest and most trusted friend. She smiled. 'I met someone in Santorini. A man.' A man whom she'd spent every night with since. His penthouse apartment or her shoebox—it didn't matter, so long as there was a bed, or a table or somewhere to lean up against while they made love.

The old man's eyes lit up. 'And this is what is putting the sparks in your eyes and the roses in your cheeks? I suspected as much.'

'It's not all down to him, I swear. Although…' Her teeth found her bottom lip as she thought back on those torrid nights. 'He's wonderful, Loukas. His name is Alexios and he's tall and handsome.'

'Alexios? So he's Greek, then? This is good. He won't be about to spirit you away from us. We don't want to lose you.'

'Stop that, Loukas!' she scolded gently. 'We've only just met. It's too early for worrying or making long-term plans.'

'Given the look in your eye, I very much doubt that. I'd say you've fallen hard. It happens that way sometimes. I'm glad for you. You've been alone too long.'

'I don't know,' she said, trying to get some sort of perspective on it now that she was back at her day job, even if she knew Alexios was waiting for her after her working day was done, and it was a miracle she could get a perspective on anything knowing what the night would bring. 'It may fizzle out, it may go nowhere, but he treats me so well. He makes me feel special. He makes me feel…' she sighed '…good about myself.'

The old man chuckled.

She laughed. 'Okay, so I sound a bit besotted. But you should meet him. You'd like him, I know.'

The old man nodded approvingly and put his gnarled-fingered hand to her shoulder. 'I am glad you have found someone special. When you have a job like ours, it is so easy to bury yourself in the past. You have to remember to live in the present. Or suddenly, when you open your eyes, you see that you are not so young any more, and that life has passed you by.'

There was a wistfulness in his words that gave them greater import. He'd rarely spoken of his private life, and she knew little about him, other than knowing he had no close family. 'Is that what happened to you? Is that why you never married?'

His retort was gruff. 'I was a fool,' he said. 'I thought I would be young for ever. I thought I had all the time in the world and that Maria would wait for me.' He raised his hands, a gesture she read as a combination of surrender and go figure. 'She didn't wait, of course. She was far more sensible than to wait for a man lost in his dusty holes in the ground. Six children, I hear she had, all grown up now and with children of their own, and she would be the best mother and *yia-yia* to each and every one of them.' He raised a wonky finger to her, the one she knew he'd broken when a rock had fallen from the walls of an excavation and crushed his hand. 'You mark my words, Athena, if you get a chance to love, then embrace it. Life is too short to waste but far too long to be busy alone.'

She pressed her lips together and nodded, moved by the sadness of his story and the scars her friend bore, scars from his dedication to his work that clearly went far beyond the physical.

'And now,' he said, stiffening his spine and slapping his knee, 'I have wasted enough time in useless reminiscences. How many divers did you say we should use?'

She put an arm around his bony shoulders and gave them a squeeze.

It took a week to assemble the necessary equipment and crew, a record time to arrange such an expedition, but the divers were happy to rearrange their schedules for such a rare find, and suppliers were for once bending over backwards to help, knowing that funding was guaranteed. Athena kept a nervous eye on the weather forecasts the entire time. If the weather held, and if the coordinates they'd been given were right, if the find was as extensive as they'd been told and if the site hadn't already been looted and the treasures of millennia lost... So many ifs, so much at stake. But it could be the crowning glory of Loukas's long and esteemed career, and the making of her own.

That was why her stomach was churning, Athena rationalised as the small expedition set off. That and the shifting sea beneath the small boats. The morning was warm, though the sun had barely risen, while the air around the team seemed to shimmer with anticipation.

The divers pulled on their masks, adjusted their regulators and, with a thumbs-up, tipped themselves backwards into the water. 'This is it,' said Loukas, with a hand to her shoulder, sounding every bit as shaky as she felt. She smiled weakly at him, her stomach roiling as she watched the gathering clouds, not wanting to put voice to her fears. Were they in the right place? Would they have time to find anything before the weather changed? Had looters already got wind and picked over the site? She took a deep gulp of the fresh sea air. No wonder she felt ill.

But one thing she was sure of—if they found anything today, she was going to do everything she could to ensure Loukas's name would be attached to the discovery for ever. Whatever it took.

Together they went into the cabin and turned their attention to the screen, where the divers' cameras were already sending images as they descended, the water growing a murkier blue, the sea floor lit with torchlight, illuminating weed-covered rocks scattered between shrubby sea plants that swayed in the shifting waters. Here and there a school of fish darted to and fro ahead of the divers.

Athena bit her lip doing her best to try to ignore the rocking movement of the vessel, her eyes scouring the seabed, searching for a sign they were in the right place. It came what felt like an entire lifetime later, despite the clock insisting only forty minutes had elapsed from the time they had begun.

'There,' she said, pointing at a corner of the screen to where it looked as if a curve of rock protruded from the sand. Covered with a thick growth of weed, it could have been exactly that, but there was something about the shape of it that drew Athena's eye and wouldn't let go. It was too perfectly formed, as if even the scum and weed of millennia were nowhere near enough to obliterate the skill of the artist who made it. 'Loukas, that could almost be the curved lip from an amphora. What do you think?'

And the older man's eyes lit up.

It was a jubilant-sounding Athena that Alexios picked up his phone to that evening, her voice competing against a background of boisterous voices and music.

'You won't believe what we found!' she

said, unable to keep the excitement from her voice, her words bubbling over each other in her rush to get them out. 'We brought up forty-six ingots and three perfect tiny amphorae that were still sealed. There were other finds too, shards of pottery and metal objects and a hundred other things we've brought back to examine besides. It was the best day.'

'Congratulations,' he said, when she finally paused long enough to take a breath.

'Forty-six ingots!' she repeated. 'The biggest find ever. Can you believe it?'

The excitement in her voice all but reached down the phone line and zapped straight into his bloodstream before heading south, as if she'd plugged a live electric wire directly into his groin, and he felt her absence from him in a rolling wave of want. He'd had her every night she'd been in Athens, tumbled her under and over him and supped deeply on her taste and her scent. But right now, what had happened in the preceding nights was irrelevant. Right now he wanted nothing more than to be in the same room as that excitement. He wanted to have her in his arms and plug himself into that intensity and feel that electric passion explode all around him.

'I have to see you.'

'I'm not sure how long we'll be here—'

He heard the noise going on behind her, music and the sound of raised, exuberant voices. 'Where are you now? I can barely hear you.'

'Celebrating with the team.' She gave him a name of a bar he knew was down near the port, but she was having to shout louder now, and he imagined her with her hand over one ear, trying to hear. He heard more laughter, and someone in the background calling her name, and he had to stop himself from growling.

Because he had the uncomfortable feeling of being cut out. Excluded from a part of her life that meant so much to her. And despite the logical part of his brain telling him that this was her work and that these were her colleagues, it didn't ease the scrape of aggravation against his raw nerve endings. But only because he was close, and he knew it. She was almost where he wanted her, and he was impatient to see this through. That was all.

'Come out for dinner with me. I'll pick you up. I want to toast your success with you.'

'I'd love that. But I have to warn you, I'm not exactly dressed for dinner.'

'Let me worry about that.'

He heard her name being called again,

more insistent this time, as a familiar tune started up in the background. 'What's happening?'

'They're dancing. They want me to join in. I should go.'

He named a time he'd pick her up and let her go.

Athena's blood was still fizzing from the excitement of the discovery and the dancing when Alexios's car pulled up outside the bar, but the fizzing ramped up tenfold even as her heart skipped a beat when Alexios unwound himself from the car. So tall and broad-shouldered, already dressed for dinner in a crisp white shirt and fitted black trousers and looking handsome as sin, the man was simply arresting.

And he'd come for her.

She put a hand to her chest in time to feel her heart kick back in again, but also a twinge, low down in her belly. About time that put in an appearance, she vaguely thought, though if her period held off a few more hours, so much the better. She had plans for this evening.

She smiled as he cut through the traffic, parting it as if he owned the road, to reach her. When had she grown so bold? It wasn't just the excitement of the discovery. It was because of Alexios, and what he'd unleashed in her. A woman wanton and reckless. A woman who wanted to give pleasure as much as taking it.

And tonight she would show him how bold she could be.

Tonight she would pleasure him.

In her cargo pants and zip-up jacket, with her hair pulled behind her head in a ponytail, she looked more like a university student than a qualified archaeologist, but whatever she looked on the surface, he knew she was all woman underneath.

She called his name as she flung herself into his arms and he used her momentum and spun her around, her joy tangible, her laughter contagious, and like a living thing. And then he put her down, and smoothed back the loose tendrils of hair where they'd whipped around her face, and dipped his mouth to kiss her smiling lips.

Theos, but she tasted good.

She tasted of sweetness and light, of dark nights and sin, and for just one moment he was thrown, because he had the oddest sensation. A memory had flitted through his mind, of coming home on a weekend from his work in the city and rounding the final bend in the windy road to catch the first view of his village, where he knew his mother and father would be waiting for him, his father tending his garden while keeping an eye out for his son, his mother cooking up his favourite dishes, *pasticcio* and *loukoumades*. It had been so many years, he'd almost forgotten what that moment had felt like.

Her eyes were bright when he gently eased away, still bubbling with joy over the successful discovery she'd made with her team this week, but, if he wasn't wrong, a good part of that wattage was down to him. That was why the feeling of coming home, he rationalised. Because soon the deathbed promise he'd made to his father would be fulfilled. Soon, the loss of his parents would be avenged.

'You wouldn't believe how special today was,' she said, sounding breathless after their kiss. 'It's the most exciting work I've ever been involved in.'

'I want to hear all about it.' And he did, if only to watch the way her mouth moved when she talked. If only to imagine those lips moving upon his. He was acutely aware their time together was growing shorter and he was determined not to miss a moment of it.

And then her smile turned to a frown as

she looked him up and down. 'But I warned you I wasn't dressed for dinner. No one will believe we're together.'

'They will once you get changed.'

'But I didn't bring—'

He stilled her mouth with a fingertip to her lips. 'I have a surprise waiting for you. Come.'

They weaved their way back to the car and within minutes Alexios was pulling up in the garage of his apartment and speeding up with her in the lift to his penthouse.

Champagne chilling in an ice bucket greeted them, and Alexios dispensed with the cork and poured them both a glass of the liquid gold. 'Congratulations,' he said, clinking his glass against hers, tasting his wine, before putting his mouth on Athena's, the bubbles sparkling as the wine swirled over their duelling tongues.

She all but melted against him in the kiss. 'That,' she said, wobbling a little, her eyelashes fluttering open, when finally they separated, 'has to be the best way to drink champagne.'

'There are other ways I can think of,' he said, and was rewarded by a smile that told him she was rapidly catching on to his wavelength. And not for the first time, it struck him that he would miss her eagerness and her enthusiasm. Earning her trust had been like unlocking the key to her sensuality. Once inside her guarded doors, he had access to her most secret places. 'But first, that surprise I told you about.' He took her hand, led her through the living room and into his bedroom where a dress he'd had delivered hung on a rack.

'I thought you might like to wear this to dinner, seeing you were feeling a little underdone.'

Athena gasped as she spied what was hanging up waiting for her. The silver-grey gown featured a beaded bodice with pearl-studded collar, with cutaways over the shoulders before falling to a high-low hemline of pleated silk. A pair of strappy sandals stood to attention below while various silken underwear and accessories were scattered on the bed.

She turned to him. 'You bought all this for me, because I had nothing suitable to wear to dinner? I could have found something remotely suitable to wear at home.'

'But where is the fun in that?' He turned her to face him and took her hands in his. 'I bought these for you, because you're worth it. Because you're a beautiful woman and

you deserve beautiful things and it makes me proud to be with you.'

'Oh, Alexios!' She pulled him closer. 'I have never, ever met anyone as amazing as you. Thank you.'

She kissed him then, open-mouthed and full of promise for the coming evening, and he felt the tug on his desire like a yank of a chain attached to his groin.

'I'll leave you to get ready,' he said, his voice gruff with want, 'but I warn you, don't keep me waiting too long, or we may not make it to dinner.'

She laughed, husky and deep, as if he wasn't the only one affected by wanting. 'I won't keep you waiting.'

True to her word, she appeared at the door a scant twenty minutes later. 'What do you think?'

'Breathtaking,' he said, and even that was an understatement. The bodice fitted her like a silver second skin leaving the smooth sweep of her shoulders bare to his gaze and to his touch, the pleated skirt floating around her legs as she moved, like the mesmerising sway of delicate sea plants under the sea, while her long hair fell in soft waves around her face. 'I think I've found the real treasure today.

You could be a mermaid from Atlantis.' His thumbs stroked the perfect skin of her shoulders, finding their way under the beaded bodice as he leaned his head close to hers and drank in her beguiling scent and the intoxicating heat of a woman.

She laughed a little. 'Then you would be a Greek god,' she countered, 'come to life. You said we made a good pair that first day we met, remember? That the world would be a safer place in our joint hands.'

His thumbs stopped moving and he pushed himself a step away. Because he remembered it all so well, the neatly laid plans, the thrill of the chase. She'd taken the bait well, believing the lies he'd spun, and now she was as good as his, and suddenly he was impatient for this game to be over.

He summoned a smile and kissed her cheek in spite of the discomfort roiling deep in his gut. Anticipation, he told himself. 'Come,' he said. 'You must be starving.'

He took her to a restaurant in the penthouse of the office block alongside his, with a view of the Acropolis where the grandiose ruins of the Parthenon glowed, beneath the temple of Athena Nike, that had set him on this course.

She was electric through the meal, lit up with the discovery and alive with it, her passion for her work, her love for uncovering the past, infusing every gesture, every word. And he couldn't help but notice that he wasn't the only man who noticed her tonight. Other men stole glances every time their partners looked away. Some openly stared at Athena, and looked at him, their lips curling in envy.

Little did they know that she would soon be available.

'Were you always like this?' he asked as she took a sip of her wine. 'So passionate about this period of history?'

She laughed then. 'No, far from it. My teenage year, for example, were a complete disaster.'

'Why?'

She shrugged, a soft shadow scudding across her eyes. 'When I was in my second-last year of high school, mum got sick. By the time she had a diagnosis, it was too late. She only had weeks to live.' She pulled a face and shrugged. 'I guess I went off the rails a bit after that. I abandoned school. My poor grandparents couldn't cope. They did the best they could but they were grieving themselves and so let me leave school, but only on the condition I came to Greece to live with my father.'

He leaned on one elbow. 'I'm sorry—about losing your mother that way.'

'Thanks,' she said, shrugging as she reached for a glass of sparkling water, taking a long swig. 'Cancer's a bitch.'

'How did it go living with your father?'

This time she managed a chuckle. 'A nightmare. Living with my father was as good as being in prison. We argued for six months about me wanting my freedom while he tried to truss me up and keep me isolated from the world, before he finally gave up and I went traveling with some of my friends. They'd finished high school and were by that time doing a gap year. And while they were living on the savings they'd put away while they studied, I had money to burn. Lots of money. Before long it wasn't just my school friends I was traveling with, I was everyone's best friend, even people I shouldn't have been, not that anyone could tell me that then.'

She took a deep breath, remembering the late-night police stations lit with cold electric light, the even colder metal benches and the long, agonising wait for rescue.

'I got in trouble—nothing too serious but, looking back, it must have been so humiliating for my father. Eventually I screwed up too many times and my father stopped send-

ing his minders to bail me out of trouble. I didn't care at the time. I was still angry at the world for losing my mother. Then one day, I got word from his lawyers that my father had disowned me. Sorry. Probably too much information. It's not a time in my life I'm particularly proud of.'

Alexios thought of the picture of her he'd seen the day he'd learned of Aristos's death, the grainy file photo of her on a boat clearly taken with a telescopic lens from a long distance away. She'd looked every bit a spoiled A-lister then, beautiful, rich and leading a self-indulgent life full of hedonistic pleasure and devoid of purpose and meaning.

That was the woman he'd been expecting to meet, and it was hard to reconcile that image of Athena with the woman she was now—passionate and driven with her work, while leading a life that couldn't be more low profile if she tried. He didn't care, of course, he was just information gathering. Waiting for the right opportunity. Waiting for the key to roll out his plans.

'So what changed?'

'I met someone.'

'What was his name?'

She laughed. 'You're so sure it was a man?'

And amusement replaced the guilt he'd heard in her voice a moment before.

'Wasn't it?'

She smiled, a knowing smile. 'It was a man, as it happens, but not in the way you think.' And he listened, as she told him of the man who'd been crouched in a fenced-off hole in the ground while she'd been traveling through Crete. She'd been walking past on her way to the beach with a group of friends, and it hadn't been the man she'd first noticed. It had been the mosaic she'd seen on the floor of the pit below—the azure blue of the recently excavated tiles, the curved sweep of the dolphins' backs, the flare of their tails and their seemingly smiling faces as they surfed the foaming waves.

Of how she'd stopped and stared, transfixed by the life in an ancient work that had lain deep below the earth for who knew how many centuries. It was only then that she'd noticed movement in the shadowed corner of the pit and she'd seen the man kneeling, gently sweeping at the newly exposed tiles with a small brush.

'Come on,' her friends had said, eager to get to the beach, already bored with the discovery.

'I'll catch up with you,' she'd said, unable

to drag herself away, before calling out to the man, 'How old is this? Do you know?'

He'd taken so long to answer, she'd thought he hadn't heard her, until slowly he'd dusted his hands on his trousers and looked up at the teenager clinging onto the rough bird-wire barrier fencing off the pit.

She remembered his wizened face and his piercing eyes, eyes that were uncannily sharp in a face leathered with time and exposure.

'Would you really like to know?' he'd asked her, and she'd nodded, and so he'd let her sit with him while he'd taken a break and told her of the ancient Minoan civilisation that had shaped and dominated the Bronze Age Mediterranean region.

She told him that, growing up in Australia, she'd only ever paid lip service to her Greek heritage and she'd found herself fascinated, entranced by an ancient civilisation that had been so cultured and advanced.

And she told him how her life had changed direction that hot afternoon. Of how she'd forgotten all about the beach and the friends waiting for her as she'd found a new purpose, and owed it all to the professor who'd taken a thread of interest and woven it into a fabric that would underpin her future life.

'I thought Loukas was an old man when I

first met him,' she said, 'and that was years ago, and he's still one of the most vital and interesting men I know I will ever meet.'

Alexios felt a stab of something like jealousy. Ridiculous when Loukas was clearly an old man. Ridiculous when Alexios didn't even care. It made no difference to him if she admired another man, if she put him on a pedestal and sang his praises.

It made no difference to him at all.

Neither did her sad tale of redemption make any difference to what he had planned.

'I've worked out a way to repay him though,' Athena continued, her features once again animated. 'I just thought of it tonight. Because there's a chronic shortage in the university and museums, and a chronic shortage of funds with which to build new facilities, and a find like today needs to be showcased somewhere special. So I'm going to fund a new wing on the museum, and dedicate it in Loukas's name.'

Alexios blinked, sitting up higher in his chair, suddenly fully invested in this conversation. 'That will cost a lot of money. Millions.'

'I don't care. I have it.'

'I know, but what if I wanted to help too? Do you think I might contribute to such a worthy cause?'

'Would you be interested?'

'I'd be honoured, if you let me donate. I don't want my name mentioned anywhere, I just want to help.'

She shook her head slightly, her smile one of wonder. 'Did anyone ever tell you, you are too good to be true?'

'No,' he said, not even trying to be modest.

But she soon would.

He signalled for the waiter, dropping a bundle of notes on the table.

'Dinner was superb, thank you,' she said as they left. 'How do you know about this place?'

'My office is right next door.'

'It is?' She glanced over at the building next door, the curtain wall of glass dark now, reflecting the street lights and the glow of the Parthenon high on the hill above. A moon had risen, hanging over the Parthenon like a giant pearl. 'Show me.'

He wasn't entirely sure if it was a question or an order, but he'd seen the spark of wickedness that had shot like a shooting star across her eyes, the spark that had mirrored his own need, and there was no way he was going to say no, not when his city apartment was ten whole minutes away. Who could wait that long?

She made small talk as he let them in, leaving the lights off, allowing the lights from the surrounding street to turn his offices into a play of grey and silver shadows and light. That silver light played over Athena, turning her from woman into goddess, prowling cat-like as if she was looking for something, glancing into cubicles, around doors, one finger trailing across a desk behind her. Conspiring with trailing the tendrils of her own special perfume—all woman, all sensuality—to lure him on.

'Impressive,' she said, walking two steps ahead of him. 'How many people did you say you employ again?'

Had he said? He couldn't remember her asking the question, let alone answering. His mind was one hundred per cent focused on one thing—to follow this game she'd started to its logical conclusion. 'Something like fifty,' he said. 'Or maybe more than, at last count.'

She turned then, and he almost bumped into her. She put a hand to his chest, a gesture that went straight to his pulsing groin. 'And where is your office?'

'This way.' He hadn't intended his voice to come out so thick around the edges, but it was as if desire had clogged his throat, just as surely as it had curdled his brain.

His office door opened with a soft snick and a small gasp. Her gasp as she took in the sight of the glowing Parthenon-topped Acropolis above. And then she was spinning around, taking it all in, the space, the view and the light. She was liquid in the light. Quicksilver in motion. Almost glowing in her joy.

She was still on the high she'd been on when he'd picked her up, so different from the woman he'd met on Santorini that day, when she'd looked as if she had the weight of the world on her shoulders.

He'd had no trouble wanting her then— she'd still been beautiful, but she'd been hurting and confused and vulnerable and he'd had a reason to seduce her—but watching her now, waiting while she absorbed the view, only ramped up his desire. And he had more of a reason now than ever. He wanted to feel her quicksilver soul all around him. He wanted to be inside her and feel her luminescent and glowing all around him.

The shadows on her face darkened, her eyes gave a wicked gleam as she turned her face to the restaurant terrace they'd just left, diners still enjoying the view and their meals. 'Can they see us?'

His arousal kicked up a notch. He liked the way she was thinking.

'Why do you ask?'

'Because you have a very big desk, Alexios,' she said, already stepping closer and curling her fingers under the waistband of his trousers, 'and I would very much like it if you made love to me on it.'

There were some things for which Alexios Kyriakos didn't need to be asked twice. Kissing a woman at sunset, when she was all warm and supple willingness in his arms, was one of them.

Making love to this woman on his desk with the gods at the Acropolis watching on added itself to the list. Shoved the others out of the way and parked itself right at the top.

His hands found her bare shoulders, sliding his fingers around to undo the collar and peel away the bodice that had separated her breasts from his gaze all night long. Not any longer.

'Not so fast,' she said, stopping his hands with hers. 'I'm still celebrating, remember?' And she dropped to her knees in front of him, her hands at his belt. 'Do you believe in luck, Alexios?'

'Not really.' Although he half suspected he was about to get lucky. 'I think people make their own luck.'

She shook her head, her fingers working at his zip. 'I'm not sure I agree, not in all cases. Because I don't think I did anything to get this lucky. I was in that café in Santorini by sheer chance and yet somehow you sat down next to me. If that isn't the most wonderful luck, I don't know what is.'

He frowned a little. That wasn't what he'd call it. 'Then you're right, it must have been luck.'

'So very lucky. And I've been thinking about this ever since that first night we spent together. I've been wanting to return the favour.'

He groaned as she released him. He groaned because release felt so good, but also because if he didn't get her on that desk, he didn't know how long he would last, and he wanted her on his desk.

Her fingers found him first, curled around and encircled him, cool and long. Air hissed through his teeth.

'My God,' she said, her breath panting words against him, 'so beautiful.'

It was then that he felt the lap of her tongue, and then another, testing his control. Tiny laps, purposeful, her tongue flicking now, testing and exploring, torture and bliss in the same carnal package.

She withdrew, giving him a chance to breathe, a moment to gasp in much-needed oxygen, and he took it. Only to feel her mouth take him in, punching the newly fought air from his lungs as her lips encircled him. Her lips sleek, a circle of warm silk, taking him deeper—so deep—into the hot cavern of her mouth, her fingers working him, cupping.

His eyes rolled back in his head, his hands fisted in her hair. She was killing him. Her lips, her tongue, her hands working in concert to bring about his end. And he wondered, with his one remaining brain cell, just who was seducing who. Because, if he didn't get her on that desk, he was a dead man.

With a superhuman effort he took her shoulders and wrenched her upright, his hands finding purchase under the firm cheeks of her behind as his mouth savaged hers, tasting the musky scent of himself on her tongue. He got her to the desk, mouths still locked as he managed to undo her collar this time, peeling her bodice down, releasing her breasts to his hands, her rock-hard nipples pressing into his palms. He groaned again, torn, as he pressed between her legs and slid the silk of her skirt up her legs.

Long legs that went on for ever.

Long, smooth legs that didn't end.

Until he suddenly realised there was no reason for them to end. No reason at all.

He groaned. 'You're not wearing any underwear.'

She lay beneath him, her legs curled around his back, her breathing ragged and hard like his, her eyes wild with want. 'See what you do to me?' she said, watching hungrily as his teeth ripped at the foil so he could roll protection on. 'See what you have turned me into?'

Her eyes flared, her back arched as his fingers tested her, finding her slick and wanting, and there was no more reason to delay.

She gasped when he filled her, shuddering around him, her muscles clenching down so hard he had to fight to pull back so he could plunge into her again, and then again, his thumb teasing her sensitive nub as the rhythm built and inexorably built.

While the gods of the Parthenon looked on, she came apart around him, electricity and magic combined in one explosive package, and, with a roar in his ears and a cry born of triumph, he shuddered his own climactic release.

He was still slumped over her on his desk, his lungs desperate to replace the oxygen he'd consumed, when she reached over to kiss his cheek. And between her own frantic breathing, she uttered the words, 'I love you.'

He stiffened at her whispered confession, the reaction so instantaneous and involuntary that he had to force himself to relax so as not to alert her.

How about that?

His plan had worked to perfection. He had the daughter of the man who had so badly wronged his father exactly where he wanted her.

It was time.

CHAPTER SEVEN

ATHENA WOKE ALONE and in her own bed to a flash of fear. Had she really confessed her love to Alexios last night?

Oh, God, she had.

But then she remembered how he'd collected her in his arms and kissed her lips and held onto her as if she was his most prized possession, and she knew he must feel something for her too.

So what that right after he'd apologised that he had an early morning meeting and that he needed to drop her home? And of course she hadn't minded. How could she? But it was the first night she'd spent alone since she'd met him, and it rammed home to her just how much she enjoyed being with him and how much she missed him when he wasn't with her. She missed seeing his sculpted face in the morning, his tousled hair, his shadowed jaw. His dark eyes watching her before he reached for her...

She shivered a delicious shiver just thinking about it. Anyway, she thought, climbing out of bed, she'd see him at lunch today to sign the paperwork. It had been his suggestion to establish a foundation to fund the new wing and it made sense to let his people prepare the paperwork. Much easier than explaining it to her lawyers, seeing as they were going into it together.

And this was on top of him wanting to contribute to the new wing in Loukas's honour—how amazing was this man? No wonder she loved him.

Meanwhile, there were treasures to record and catalogue.

It was only when she got to the bathroom that she felt a bit queasy. The morning after, she figured—it had been a night of celebration, after all. But she had far too much on today to let a hangover get in her way, so she pushed through her queasiness and got ready for work.

It was going to be a good day.

He stood at his window, looking up at the Acropolis, while the stack of papers sat ready on his desk. All it required was a few signatures and it would be done. Sweat lined his top lip while his heart thumped loudly in his ears and the serpent in his gut fed on his anticipation and coiled and writhed. Ten years of planning, ten years of building so he would be in a position to avenge his father, was about to come to fruition.

Ten years.

'You should never have betrayed my father, Stavros Nikolides,' he hissed, through a too tight jaw. 'You were never going to get away with that.'

Even death hadn't saved him.

Because now the daughter would pay for the sins of the father.

Athena.

He would miss her.

The thought came from nowhere, so unexpected that it jolted him into motion. He turned away from the window and looked back at the waiting papers, topped with a page headed *'Fund for the Establishment of the Loukas Spyrides Wing'*. That paper did what it said on the box, and neatly hid all the pages below that would result in an entirely different outcome from that which she was expecting.

No, he would miss the sex. Would miss the look on her face when she hovered on the edge before exploding around him. Would miss her in his bed. Would miss her body within easy reach. That was all.

He thought about her last night, splayed out on his desk—this desk—thought about her whispered confession.

'I love you.'

And he turned away again, the serpent tying his gut into knots.

She wouldn't love him for long. She would hate him after this, and little wonder. That would spell the end of her inhabiting his bed.

Collateral damage.

But what did it matter? It wasn't as if he cared what she thought of him. He wasn't about to get sentimental, not now. What he cared about was that his plan was ready to be carried out. It was what he'd worked for this last ten years after all. Ten long years. And if he didn't have this, then what had he been working towards? What was the point of his life?

No, when he was so close to avenging his father, so close to making good on his death-bed promise, there was no going back.

His phone buzzed. 'Yes?'

'She's here,' Anton said.

The serpent in his gut pulled tight.

'Send her in.'

* * *

'So many papers to sign,' Athena said, as Alexios flipped to the next sticky note. He'd been through the pages of the first paper with her, explaining how the fund would be set up and operated, and she'd nodded her agreement with the arrangements. The rest of it, he'd explained, was all formalities and authorities to act on behalf of the fund.

'You know what lawyers are like,' he said, 'always wanting to dot every "i" and cross every "t".'

'That's true,' she said, signing her name yet again before Alexios flipped over more pages to the next sticky note. 'I couldn't believe the amount of paperwork the lawyers shoved in front of me the day I learned about my inheritance.'

'And that's it,' said Alexios, after one more signature, scooping up the papers from the desk in front of her, and tapping them briefly on the desk before tucking them into a folder and out of sight.

'That's a relief,' she said, putting the pen down. 'I was getting writer's cramp. Do you have a copy for me to take to my lawyers?'

'No need for that. I've already arranged to have it scanned and sent straight through.'

She smiled. 'Thank you. It sounds like you've thought of everything.'

'Yes,' he said unable to stop himself smiling in return. 'I believe I have. Do you have to rush off back to work?'

She glanced at her watch and stood. 'I really should. There's so much work to do on the find.' Her tongue found her top lip and she frowned a little. 'Loukas would like us to put in some extra time to get everything catalogued. It might mean a few late nights, starting tonight. Do you mind if we skip dinner?'

He put his arm around her shoulders to walk her to the door, torn between disappointment and relief. He wouldn't have minded one last night with her—a farewell tour of all his favourite places—but maybe it was better to make a clean break now. After all, what kind of low-life would he be if he'd stolen her fortune and then slept with her? He pressed his lips to her brow and breathed her scent for what would be the last time. 'I guess I have to get used to sharing you with success. I'll stop distracting you and let you concentrate on your discoveries—and maybe let you get some sleep in the process.'

She smiled up at him. 'Sleep would be a change.' Such a beautiful face, she had. So open. So trusting now, with no hint of the caution and suspicion she'd shown that first day. She waved her hand in the direction of the desk where the signed papers lay. 'When do you think we'll hear more from the lawyers?'

'It won't take long. I expect we'll hear of any developments tomorrow.' *If not sooner.*

'So soon?' She reached up on tippy toes and pressed her lips to his. 'Thank you so much for doing this for me. You're the best.'

Then she was gone.

Alexios flopped into his chair, staring blindly out of the window, waiting for the feeling of exhilaration to kick in. The feeling of exhilaration he was owed. Because he'd done it, hadn't he? He'd made good on the deathbed promise he'd made his father.

It was done.

But instead of exhilaration, he felt—numb. No doubt because he'd spent so long on this journey and now the final blow had been struck. The share transfers she'd blindly signed over to his name would be filed today and by tomorrow every bit of the Nikolides empire would be his.

There was a knock on the door and Anton entered. 'You have the signatures?' Without turning, Alexios picked up the folder, pulled the first few pages from the file, and held the folder out for him. 'Like plucking ripe fruit from the tree,' he said.

'And she suspected nothing?' his co-con-spirator said, taking the folder and flicking through the pages.

'Not a thing,' said Alexios, as he tore the Loukas Spyrides Fund agreement into tiny pieces and let them scatter on the floor around him. 'Not a thing.'

Loukas smiled when Athena returned from her lunchtime appointment with Alexios. 'You look happy.'

She stashed her handbag and smiled right back. 'It was a good lunch, thank you.' Even though she hadn't eaten a thing.

The old man chortled, and Athena turned a piercing eye at him. 'And that's all I'm telling you.'

Because she wasn't telling him anything yet. The Loukas Spyrides Wing was her surprise to him, a thank you for all he'd done in her life, but she wanted to wait until everything and all the approvals were in place and the plans under way. Then she'd organise an evening to honour her mentor and make the announcement.

'But I will be working late tonight,' she said, 'so there's that.'

He clapped her on the shoulders as he passed. 'I'm so sorry to keep you from the man you love.'

'It's not for long,' she said, not bothering to argue when she knew what he said was true. 'And this is a labour of love.'

'I've made a fresh pot of coffee,' Loukas said, on his way to the kitchen. 'Can I get you one?'

And Athena said yes, until he put the freshly brewed coffee on her desk and her stomach churned as she caught a whiff. She put a hand to her mouth. Oh, boy.

'Are you all right?'

She couldn't answer. She dared not open her mouth. It was all she could do to flee to the rest rooms before she lost what little contents were in her stomach.

It seemed to take for ever, the heaving, the violent retching, and yet it was only a matter of minutes before she was staring into the mirror, pressing wet towels against her blotched face, the eyes staring back at her looking frightened.

Because this could be no reaction to last night's overindulgence. Not when her cramps had still not seen a period arrive. She'd blamed it on her irregular period, but she'd felt queasy on the boat that day, too...

God, it couldn't mean... She couldn't be—could she?

Surely not! That wasn't supposed to happen. Alexios had used condoms, hadn't he?

She squeezed her eyes shut.

Except for that one time.

Oh, God, that time on the boat, when he'd asked her afterwards if she'd been safe and she'd misunderstood and said yes...

How could she tell him the truth, after telling him that she was? And even though she loved him, it was still too new. There was still so much they had to learn about each other. Still so much they didn't know.

Though he'd admitted he would like a family one day...

She took a deep breath and wiped her face one final time.

And even if Alexios had stayed silent after her clumsy declaration of love last night, even if he hadn't told her he loved her too—he did care for her. He must—otherwise why would he want to get involved with jointly funding the new wing? If she was pregnant—and it was still only if—then she would go see him and she would explain. She trusted him. He would understand.

Loukas hovered over her when she got

back. 'You look so pale. Something's wrong—you should see a doctor.'

'I will,' she agreed, knowing she was letting Loukas down, but her stomach was still feeling queasy and she knew she was as much as useless today. She would see a doctor if it came to that, but first of all she would call in to a *pharmakeia* on the way home—if only to obtain the tools to rule the possibility out.

She didn't wait for morning, as the box suggested. She couldn't. She had to know. She tore open the box and the packaging and followed the instructions, praying that her period would miraculously appear and that she'd wasted her money while she held her breath for the allotted time.

The packaging lied. The stick took nowhere near the allotted time. Two bold blue lines screamed out at her.

She was pregnant.

Pregnant with Alexios's child.

She stayed there, staring at the stick and sitting on the pan, because her legs were suddenly worse than useless. And she didn't feel nauseous any more, so much as blindsided. Steamrollered.

Pregnant.

The word held a world of connotations and

consequences and none of them she could get her head around.

Pregnant.

What the hell would it mean for her work—her career? She was just getting started in her professional career. She hadn't figured on children until her thirties at least, and then, only vaguely, as something that might happen in the future.

And what would it mean for her and Alexios? She put a hand low down over her belly where a baby was already growing. Her baby.

God, what the hell was she going to do?

She didn't know. All she knew was that she couldn't deal with this on her own. She had to talk to Alexios. She had to tell him.

Resolve poured strength back into her legs and got her moving. She was almost out of the door when her phone rang. The lawyers' number, she recognised. They hadn't wasted any time. Probably just confirming receipt of the signed documents.

She listened, but the speaker's voice was too loud and garbled, almost manic, for her to be able to make any sense out of what was being said—something about shares? But that made even less sense.

'*Signome,*' she said to him in Greek.

'Please, slow down. I don't understand. These are the signed papers to establish the Loukas Spyrides Fund?'

The man at the end of the line cursed and seemed to take great delight from telling her he had no idea what she was talking about. He was talking about the papers she'd signed handing over a hundred per cent ownership and control of the Nikolides Group to Alexios Kyriakos.

And Athena's knees buckled under her.

CHAPTER EIGHT

IT WAS A MISTAKE. Athena took a taxi to Alexios's offices. He wasn't expecting her, but he'd see her, she knew. This was too important for him not to. Because the lawyer had to be mistaken. She'd signed papers establishing a fund for a new wing in Loukas's honour, nothing about shares. She'd read through the first pages herself—she knew what she'd signed.

Although there had been an awful lot of documents...

What if...?

She chewed her bottom lip, her mind tangled in possibilities.

No, it wasn't possible. Alexios wouldn't do such a thing. It was unthinkable. She'd see him. He'd soon get to the bottom of it.

The taxi driver stopped at a red light and Athena almost screamed at him to ignore it, so impatient was she to get to Alexios's offices. This wasn't the impromptu visit to Alexios she'd anticipated, filled with trepidation and nervous tension at sharing her news with him, wondering how it would be received. Instead she felt confused, baffled, because it couldn't be happening—but what if it was?

Finally they were there. She thrust a pile of euros at the driver when he pulled up, not bothering to wait for her change, arriving breathlessly at the front desk. 'I need to see Alexios.'

The receptionist recognised her from her earlier visit and smiled, reaching for her phone. 'Do you have an appointment?'

She shook her head. 'Alexios will see me.'

He had to.

'She's downstairs.' Anton put the phone down. 'Do you want to see her?'

So the shit had already hit the fan? So be it. Alexios had told her it wouldn't take long to hear from her legal team but even he was surprised at their efficiency. He smiled. The lawyers for the Nikolides Group must be running around like headless chickens right now.

And Athena must be reeling. No doubt, she wouldn't believe it until she heard it from him. Alexios sighed as he stood and strode to the windows, to the view out to the Parthenon. 'I suppose it's unavoidable. Send her in.'

'Alexios!'

Athena rushed past Anton at the door, but something about Alexios stopped her halfway over to him. He was standing by the window, arms crossed, with the sun poking out from behind a cloud behind him, his body in silhouette. While she stood rooted to the spot, he turned around, his arms still crossed. 'You wanted to see me?'

She couldn't see his face, but his tone was all wrong, his body language all wrong, and there was a vibe coming from him that charged the air and spoke of danger. The hairs on the back of her neck prickled. 'Alexios?'

He said nothing. He didn't make a move towards her, and Athena felt as if she were being sucked into some parallel universe, where everything she thought she knew was suddenly back to front and upside down, and somehow she'd wandered into the wrong office of the wrong Alexios. She swallowed down against a rising tide of panic and a bitter taste in her throat. Because things couldn't be that wrong.

'I had a call from my lawyers,' she said.

'I told you you'd soon be hearing from them.'

The tone of his voice was strangely at odds

with the rest of him. It was almost as if he were talking to a child, the verbal equivalent of a pat on the head, but there was no comfort there. No solace. It almost felt as if there were a crack in the air between them and it was widening with every passing second. 'But they said they knew nothing about a fund for the new Loukas wing.'

'You signed those papers yourself.'

'I know, but...' She paused, willing him to fill in the gaps, to tell her there must have been some mistake and that he would soon sort it out. 'That's what I didn't understand. Because they said, and I know it sounds crazy—they said something about the ownership of the Nikolides Group being transferred to you.' She gave a little laugh. No more than a bubble of sound that no sooner swirled into the fractured room and died a quicker death than if it had been made from soap. 'Because that's crazy, isn't it?'

'Maybe it's time you put her out of her misery,' came a voice behind her. 'Maybe it's time you told her the truth.'

She spun around. She hadn't realised the man was still in the room. She turned back to Alexios and put out her arms in appeal. 'What does he mean—tell me the truth? Alexios, what's going on? I don't understand.'

He moved then, but not to her. He moved to his desk—the desk that they'd made love on under the silvery light of the moon—and sprawled down in his chair. Now she could see his face, and yet he was almost unrecognisable. His features looked twisted, a snarling animal in the place of the man she thought she knew.

Her heartbeat spiked, because for the first time she didn't just feel confused, she felt afraid.

'Alexios?' she whispered. 'Tell me it's not true.'

'You really should be more careful what you put your signature to, Athena.'

'What? You went through those papers with me. I signed papers to establish a fund—we both did.'

There was a snigger from behind her. 'And underneath those? Did you not realise you were signing your fortune away?'

The realisation was like a sucker punch to her gut. She gasped, almost doubled over, while blood pounded in her ears. Still she was unable to tear her eyes from Alexios's suddenly twisted face, willing him to deny it, to say it had all been a horrible mistake. But he didn't even try to deny it.

When finally she could find the words, her

voice sounded as if it were coming from a long, long way away. Another world. Another time. 'So it's true.'

But it was as if she hadn't spoken. All he said was, 'Leave us, Anton.'

'And miss the fireworks when we've worked on this so long?'

'Get out!'

She turned as the door behind her opened, and Anton went, but not before he'd taken one last look over his shoulder at her, one last sneer, giving her one last glance of profile.

She blinked, remembering in a thunderbolt that momentarily blinded her as realisation zapped down her spine and out to her extremities. A café in Santorini. A man with her bag under his arm, looking back at her to see if he was being followed.

She turned back to Alexios, white-cold fury running thick like mercury in her veins, pieces emerging from the tumult of her mind and fitting together in a horrible new way. 'Him,' she said, and she could see by the flare in Alexios's eyes that she was right. 'It was him all along. You had your goon steal my bag that night so I would, what? Feel indebted so I would agree to have dinner with you? Because I owed you, my champion, my knight in shining armour? My hero? You planned it all, every last detail. The bag-snatching, the dinner waiting. Did you plan for me to fall into your bed? Was your seduction part of that plan too?'

'A not unpleasant part.'

She swept his words away as despair crashed over her in a wave that threatened to bring her undone. 'You must have been so sure of yourself—every step planned—every detail worked out to the nth degree, and all the time you were dragging me deeper and deeper into the web you spun. A web made of lies!'

Tears coursed down her cheeks, hot and angry, the salt stinging her eyes, but she didn't bother to wipe them away. There was no pretending and she couldn't stop. 'And like a fool I fell for it. I fell for you. I trusted you. I trusted you!' Her lips tightened. She had to bite down hard against the urge to sob. She couldn't break down now, not before she got out the words she needed to say. 'I even thought I loved you—but you were a liar from the very beginning. You were a liar all along. You disgust me.'

He stood, half turning to gaze out of the windows. 'If that's all, I see no reason to extend this meeting. I think it's time you left.'

She stayed right where she was. Anger

was taking root in her veins now. Cold, hard anger, and she would not be summarily dismissed, not like some inconsequential employee. Not before he gave her some kind of explanation for his treachery. 'Why, Alexios? I don't understand. Why would you do such a thing? Why would you go to such lengths?'

'Maybe you should ask your father.'

'But you know... My father is dead.'

'Hnh.' He turned back, turned the emptiest and bleakest eyes she'd ever witnessed back on her. 'You see? You're already working it out. And now, if that's all?'

His words made as much sense as his actions, but it was clear that his cryptic words were all the explanation she would get. She kicked her chin up high. 'I'll go,' she said. 'I can't bear to be in the same room with you a moment longer. I can't bear to breathe the same air.'

She slammed the door behind her so hard every head swivelled her way. She looked dreadful, she knew, but she didn't bother wiping her tear-streaked face or blowing her dripping nose, not when she had more important things on her mind.

Because her world was falling apart, shattering, unravelling, and she didn't understand how it could have happened. She didn't understand any of it.

Like slops from a bucket, she spilled out of the building and onto the streets of Athens, and found the nearest rubbish bin to cling to while she heaved out her empty stomach and aching heart.

For a long time Alexios stood at the window staring up at the Acropolis, watching the moving ants that were tourists scurrying around the ruins, looking for scraps of the past before they scurried back to their buses and on to the next site and their next ten minutes of history.

But it wasn't the tourists causing the coiling, snaking feeling in his gut. It was Athena.

He'd expected her to be upset.

He'd expected her to be angry. Why wouldn't she be both upset and angry when she'd gone from pauper to billionaire and back to pauper almost before the ink was dry on her father's will?

He'd expected her to be hurt. Baffled. Confused. But how could he avenge her father's betrayal of his father without hurting her? What she didn't realise was that it wasn't about her.

Collateral damage.

It wasn't personal.

And there was no feeling guilty and no

point trying to explain it, because it didn't matter if she understood or not. It didn't matter if she was angry and confused and hurt. All that mattered was that it was done.

He slammed his palm against the glass and slammed shut the door on his emotions. Curse the woman to hell and back, but he would not feel guilty!

He sucked in air as he glanced at his watch, telling himself to forget about Athena, because there was something more important he had to do. If he left now, he would be there before dark.

Athena somehow managed to stumble home. She must have looked a sight staggering blindly through streaming eyes down the streets, but she couldn't pull herself together, couldn't pretend she wasn't shattered. Everything her father had left her—the houses, the businesses—it was all gone. But it wasn't the loss of her fortune that caused her the most distress. It was the betrayal of the man she'd grown to love.

The man who was the father of her child.

She collapsed onto her bed and let the tears fall into her pillow—desperate tears, futile tears—until finally her tears ran dry. Because all the tears in the world wouldn't change anything. She'd had such high hopes. Happy hopes. She'd been so excited to tell Alexios her news. But instead of joy, all Alexios had caused her was heartbreak. And still none of it made any sense. Still, she couldn't understand why he'd done what he'd done.

All she understood was that once again she was alone in the world. Alone, but for this tiny seed growing inside her.

She rolled onto her back feeling drained and exhausted, her eyes puffy and aching, and spread her hand low over her belly. It would serve him right if she decided not to go ahead with the pregnancy, if she decided to destroy something of his life when he had so thoroughly destroyed hers.

It would serve him right when she still didn't know how she was supposed to cope with a baby, let alone all by herself.

Her fingers curled, her fingernails digging into her belly, as if she could simply pluck it out.

It would serve him right!

But where was the satisfaction in doing that when Alexios would never learn what she had done, or what he had lost?

Besides, could she really do such a thing? She swallowed, burying her first impulse to strike back at him the only way she could, when she thought about what was involved. It would never be as simple as it sounded. There would be all kinds of medical appointments and a visit to the sterile antiseptic environs of a clinic where her baby's brand-new life would be snuffed out. And there would be the aftermath, when she thought about what she had done and wondered—a boy or a girl? There would be a due date that would never be—a constant reminder—a birthday with never a celebration.

Her heart squeezed tight and fresh tears welled in her eyes.

Poor baby. Poor helpless baby. How could she take Alexios's betrayal out on something so tiny? So innocent? So utterly dependent on her for its survival.

She rolled over onto her side and buried her weeping face in her pillow. She couldn't, that was how.

She would have this baby to spite him. She would bring it up surrounded by love and safe from fathers who didn't know what love was.

And Alexios could go to hell, but he would never hear her news.

Never know that he was going to be a father.

The mountain winds were brutal and whipped around Alexios's collar, tugging at the hem of his coat as he put the small bunch of flowers down, while scattered gravestones appeared and disappeared in the swirling mist, glowing ghostly white in the eerie light before vanishing again. But Alexios didn't flinch. The wind didn't bother him. The gloom and the mist didn't spook him. His focus was fixed on the gravestone before him, the simple cross that bore his family name, and the names of his mother and father.

He knelt there, in the damp earth before the grave, his thoughts swirling like the mist that surrounded him. He thought about the promise he had made to a dying man, about the fire in his belly that had burned since that day. That had possessed him for so many years.

But his thoughts kept getting interrupted by images of a woman with confusion and hurt in her eyes, a woman who had no right to be in his thoughts at all, a woman who had no place here, amongst the people her father had hurt the most.

He shook his head, trying to rid his mind of the pictures of her. To rid himself of this ceaseless gnawing at his gut. Because he'd achieved what he'd promised his father, hadn't he? It wasn't for guilt that he'd lived and worked and burned every day since.

His fingers clenched and unclenched by his sides while he stared at the simple grave, remembering the promise he'd made to a dying man all those years ago, the promise made good.

'It is done,' he said, the words plucked from his mouth and carried away on the biting wind. 'It is done.'

There was no bolt of lightning to accompany his words. No thunderclap or sudden clearing of the mist to signal the fatal blow to the Nikolides Group that Alexios had struck today. No acknowledgment from the heavens to celebrate the achievement of a decade-long dream.

The mist continued to swirl and the wind still whipped around him with icy tentacles, but, instead of a sense of victory, it was the crack inside him he felt, the crack that kept shifting, grinding its slow way open.

Because in that moment, he wondered, where was the satisfaction? He wondered what it was all for.

'If it brought you back,' he said, struggling through a throat clogged tight. 'If it made a difference.'

But he knew that it couldn't. He knew that it wouldn't.

And wasn't that the greatest blow of all?

So with one final nod of his head, he turned away from the gravestones and let the swirling mist reclaim them.

It took two days before she could manage to drag herself out of bed and front up to work, and she knew that if she hadn't had her work, and if she hadn't had this baby growing inside her, she would have had no reason to get up at all.

It was Loukas who got her through those first few agonising days, Loukas who provided a shoulder for Athena to cry on in the next few weeks after that, while together they worked on the paper they were preparing to announce the discovery. It was Loukas who was only too willing to listen when she needed to confide in someone, or chose to stay silent when she couldn't bear to discuss it. Her old friend and mentor was the crutch she needed to lean on, circling warily around her at work, trying not to fuss but looking worried for her nonetheless.

'Tea,' he offered now, his gentle smile widening when she realised he'd lifted his head from his own work and been watching her staring into space.

Athena nodded her thanks and smiled back, before Loukas disappeared with their mugs to the rudimentary kitchen. She heard the sound of water running, the snap of the lid closing and the flick of the power switch.

She smiled as she heard her old friend muttering as he fiddled with tea bags and battled to open the ancient fridge. After four weeks, Loukas was still acutely worried about her, surrounding her in a cotton-wool dressing, and it occurred to her that so long as Loukas was around, she wasn't as alone as she'd always imagined herself.

But he didn't have to worry about her. Time was her opportunity to look back, to make sense of what had happened, and the more time that passed, the more sense things made.

From the very beginning, she'd been suspicious of Alexios's motives. Cautious. She'd been right to be as it turned out. But because he'd always been one step ahead, he'd drawn her in, like a bird tempted to follow a trail of breadcrumbs.

Mikro peristeri.

His little dove.

His *stupid* little dove.

He'd had her bag snatched so he could save the day. He'd offered to leave the gate of the palace in Santorini unlocked, so she felt safe. He'd let her think he wasn't stopping her from leaving, when she'd expected him to try something—anything—during that amazing sunset. And because he hadn't, she'd been left wanting.

And when she'd told him she was leaving, that a shipwreck had been discovered and she had to go, he'd protested, and she'd been flattered that she'd meant something to him. But he'd said, *'It doesn't have to end now.'*

At the time she'd thought nothing of his use of that little word—*now.*

But in hindsight, it made perfect, dreadful sense. Without her realising, he'd hinted at the ugly truth of what he'd intended all along. Because he'd always known it was going to end; that had been his plan the whole time, to steal her fortune and to cut her loose.

He'd snatched her fortune as easily as he'd snatched her bag.

God, she'd been so naïve, so ripe for the picking.

She gulped down air that tasted of betrayal and injustice and one thousand regrets, as freshly pressed as that very first day, and for a moment felt swamped by it.

But damn him to hell and back, she would not drown under the torrent of emotion. She would not be broken, least of all by him.

What bothered her more was that now there would be no Professor Loukas Spyr-

ides Wing of the museum to show off the
treasures they'd recovered from their watery
grave. That bit stung so much, and the only
consolation was that she'd never told Loukas
what she'd planned for him, so he didn't have
to be disappointed too.

She curled her open hand over her belly
under which their baby lay. *No.* No longer
their baby. *Her* baby. Alexios had given up
any and all rights to this child when he had
done the unthinkable and taken her trust, and
thrown it back in her face.

And no, she wasn't worried any more. She
was angry and she was resolute. Determined.
She would be strong for herself and her growing baby.

She just wished being strong would help
take the pain away. She'd thought love would
die a quick death. She'd imagined it had died
those first days when she was so stunned and
angry and blindsided and numb.

She'd willed it to die.

But love wasn't as simple as that, she'd
learned. Love was illogical. Irrational. Discomfiting and inconvenient. Love stuck like
glue, even when hate did its best to dislodge it.
Love stuck around, even when circumstances
dictated that it had no right to be there.

Alexios had no claim on her heart. Not

now. But still her heart didn't listen. Still it subjected her to sleepless nights reliving his lovemaking. Remembering how tender he'd been. How precious he'd made her feel.

Because he'd lied so well? Or because he'd actually felt a shred of something for her?

She shook her head. Clearly because he'd lied so well. She couldn't afford to dwell on the alternative—she'd lose her sanity if she went down that route, and already she'd lost too much.

'Athena,' said Loukas softly when he returned, obviously interpreting the tortured thoughts reflected on her face. 'I know it's not my place to say this, but you know, if it makes you so miserable, you don't have to have the baby.' And then a moment later he shook his head. 'I'm sorry. It's none of my business. Please forget I said anything.'

She reached out a hand to him. 'It's okay, Loukas. I did think about it. I seriously considered it. But I kept thinking, it's not the baby's fault. Why should the baby have to pay the price of its mother's mistake?'

He nodded then, his eyes dewy, and put his gnarled hand over hers. 'I understand. One day you will find someone who truly deserves you, someone who loves you and your child.'

She shook her head. 'You know, I don't think I'll do that at all. With the example my parents set me, I don't think I'd be very good at it.'

'There is nothing written in the stars that says your own marriage couldn't be very different.'

'Maybe not, but it's the only marriage I've ever seen up close, and it wasn't pretty. I think I'd rather pass than inflict that on myself and a child.'

'You can't say that now. You can't predict what will happen.'

'We'll see. But what I do know is that, growing up, all I ever wanted was my father to love me.' She shrugged. 'I honestly don't think he was capable of the emotion. And I know he never wanted me. My mother dying was an inconvenience, because then I became an inconvenience.

'But I'm determined that that is never going to happen to this child. I'm going to be both mother and father to it, and it is never going to wonder if it is wanted or loved.'

He smiled as he patted her hand. 'This is one very lucky child, to have you for its mother.'

Alexios stepped from the helicopter, his thumping heart challenging the rotors for ascendancy as he set foot on the island for which his father had held such high hopes. If he'd needed a reminder of why he'd done what he'd done, a reminder of why he'd planned and schemed for ten long years to take over the Nikolides empire, here it was. Argos island—site of his father's dream, a source of so much hope, of an island respite for his hard-working village colleagues.

Argos island, that instead had delivered so much grief over the years.

All because of Stavros Nikolides and his insatiable greed.

He sucked in a breath flavoured with avgas and vengeance in equal parts and, *Theos*, it tasted as good as he'd always imagined it would.

He walked along the tiled path climbing to the house, shrubs of wild thyme seasoning the warm salt air, a cluster of olive trees clinging to a hillside, while crowning it all spread the house, long and white and bold against a brilliant blue sky.

Blessed by nature and surrounded by the stunning Aegean waters with stunning views to the mainland, the island itself was a jewel. No wonder his builder father had seen such potential here.

Then he looked closer at the white palace—

the abomination that Stavros had built—sprawling over the top of the island as if it were clutching it, laying claim to it—a palace for one man who had found it impossible to share.

He stood on the bridge over the infinity pool that ran the length of the house, so that every room on this side opened onto it, and found himself wondering about Athena. Had she swum in this pool and spent days lazing by its side? And then he turned away, pushing aside that unwelcome thought with it. It was enough to know that no Nikolides would ever be swimming here again.

White curtains billowed at the sides of doors thrown open by the housekeeper in preparation for Alexios's arrival, their nervous fluttering like excited schoolchildren anticipating their first day with a new teacher.

He ventured inside, across the marble-lined entry, so large it could be a reception room in its own right, and through into what could only be described as a ballroom, it was so enormous. Marble again lined the walls and floors and the large square columns that held up the ceiling weighted down with massive crystal chandeliers. Two white leather couches were perched at one end of the room, a white rug separating them, while massive mirrors were fixed to opposite walls, reflecting all that marble magnificence and then reflecting the reflections, so it looked as if the room went on for ever in both directions.

His footsteps echoed in the empty spaces as he moved from room to room. Every room in this ice palace was too big, the furnishings too garish and opulent. It was hideous, multi-levelled, and so many self-contained wings spread out behind it was like a cancer creeping across the island.

Like the cancer that had killed his mother because his father hadn't been able to afford her treatment...

His hands fisted at his sides.

So much grief. So much heartache. It was good he had come. It made it real, what he had achieved. What he had won back for his father.

He would fix it, this marble and mirrored monstrosity. He would have it toned down, injected with some warmth, and set up to be a holiday-break destination. The village had moved on since his father's time. Families had moved away, seeking work in the cities. Sons and daughters had gone to university and found work elsewhere. But there were still plenty of people doing it tough. People who could never afford to take a break from their lives. The Kostas Foundation would find them. It always had, people like Anton who'd been sleeping on the streets from the time his mother had abandoned him at six years of age. Kids who'd grown up street smart but education poor. Kids who courted with crime, skirting around the boundaries of the law-abiding population, on a daily basis.

He could make it happen.

And finally he could bring his father's dreams to life, or at least a version of them. It was something.

He cast a glance at the pool as he strode back on his way to the helicopter, imagining a younger version of Athena splashing around in the pool, feeling an unexpected stab of guilt. What was she doing now? Licking her wounds with her colleagues? Crying over her spilt fortune?

He shook his head and looked around at the island, already eager to get the plans for its transformation under way. It was a shame, that was all. He'd enjoyed having Athena in his bed, but it couldn't be helped. He shouldn't feel guilty.

CHAPTER NINE

Two months later...

ALEXIOS DIDN'T SPEND a lot of time at the Kostas Foundation School. He attended all the necessary board meetings, of course, and he'd visit at Easter and Christmas when the kids put on an assembly and some kind of performance, but he didn't tend to drop in uninvited. Which was why the principal was so surprised to see him when he called by unexpectedly.

'Mr Kyriakos,' he said, as he extended a hand to welcome his visitor. 'We weren't expecting you. To what do we owe this pleasure?'

Alexios shook it. 'I won't take much of your time, Con. Just want to see how my money is being put to good use.'

'I think there's no question of that,' the principal said, his chest puffing out in pride, clearly delighted at his surprise guest, already gesturing him to the door. 'How about I give you a tour and show you?'

He led Alexios through the hallways of the building that had been an orphanage in days gone by, until the supply of unwanted babies had dried up and the buildings had lain unwanted and neglected. Until Alexios had found the mouldering property, and decided the big rooms, sleeping quarters and huge kitchen would be perfect for a school, for street kids who had nowhere to live and nothing in their bellies and no chance of an education that didn't involve learning how to break the law and get away with it. Street-smart kids who could make it in the world and become useful citizens, if only they could see another way to survive and prosper. Kids whose futures weren't determined by destiny, but by opportunity. Kids who could benefit from the lessons he'd learned along the way, transforming himself from a dirt-poor village kid to a billionaire.

The principal showed Alexios around the classrooms, where he saw the students, aged from six to sixteen, and all variously engaged in doing their sums or reading the classics, and learning life skills too for the older kids, like how to open a bank account, handle a job interview, even things like how to negotiate a deal.

Then they stopped by the gleaming kitchen, where meal after meal was prepared, to be fallen upon by the hungry students who would otherwise have to beg or steal for food on the unforgiving streets of Athens. They toured the hostel, where sometimes for the first time in their lives, the kids had a bed and a room of their own.

And the more they toured, the more the spiked cannonball that had been rolling around in his gut these past few weeks lost its sharp barbs. The more his mind eased. By the time he left, he knew he wasn't a bad person, even though that cannonball had been rolling around puncturing his gut ever since he performed his coup and claimed the Nikolides fortune for his own—and leaving a trail that might have been written in Braille, that said bad. Evil.

But today's visit had proved he wasn't a bad person. Not really. Whatever Athena thought of him now.

Because it wasn't as if he'd wanted to relieve Athena of her fortune because he'd envied or lusted after her money and wanted it for his own. It wasn't because of anything she'd done.

It was because of Stavros, and what he'd done, and the promise Alexios had made to him on his father's deathbed.

It had nothing to do with Athena herself.

It wasn't personal.

He just had to keep reminding himself of that.

By the time Alexios returned to his office, the boost in his spirits was already wearing thin. He cursed as he flopped into his chair, spinning away from his desk to gaze unseeing out of the windows. He'd known it wouldn't last, of course, it never did. That was the trouble he was having lately. Nothing satisfied him. Nothing could take away this lingering dissatisfaction, and the annoying thing was he couldn't pin it down to anything. He was just unsettled. Unsatisfied. It made no sense given he was busier than ever. He had a new empire to get to know and to oversee. He had a new fortune to manage.

And yet it wasn't enough.

It felt as though he had achieved a life-long ambition and there was no other reason to go on, no other goal to pursue.

Anton buzzed his phone and Alexios almost ignored him. The man had become unbearable lately. Smug and supercilious, as if he had single-handedly pulled off the coup of the century. But the man had his uses. He picked up.

'*Ne?*'

'There's news,' Anton said, and the unveiled delight in his voice was enough to alert Alexios that this was news about Athena.

'What?' he snapped impatiently. Because if it was more of the same, more of the news that she looked like death as she shuffled between her squalid apartment and her job at the department, he didn't need to hear it. He didn't need the added dose of guilt.

'She's got an appointment tomorrow with a doctor. A specialist.'

Alexios sat at attention, his ears pricked up. 'What kind of specialist?'

'An obstetrician,' Anton said, pausing a moment to let that sink in. 'A baby doctor. It appears that your ex-girlfriend is pregnant.'

Pregnant.

A tidal wave of shock surged up inside him, swamping his senses and his mind, obliterating his earlier funk.

'A new boyfriend?'

'Still nobody. She goes to work, goes home, that's it.'

Blood roared in Alexios's ears. Because Athena was pregnant and it could only mean one thing. It was his baby.

His child.

He couldn't stay seated. He had to stand, a feeling like victory flowing through his veins, forcing him to move. To act. It was more than he could have dreamed possible. It was a gift from the gods, making up for stealing his thunder by rudely taking Stavros before Alexios had time to get even.

Because he hadn't just succeeded in bedding Stavros's daughter—Alexios had planted her with his seed.

He smiled as Anton filled him in on the details of the appointment, sparing a moment for the man who had done his father so wrong. It was beyond perfect. Stavros mustn't just be turning in his grave, he must be spinning.

Bracing herself against the cold wind channelling between the buildings, she dodged awkwardly through the crowds crossing the busy street, wishing she'd not had to drink and hold quite so much water, but both excited and a little bit nervous for her twelve-week scan. This was not the way Athena would have preferred to have a baby, as a single woman negotiating the entirely new learning curve of pregnancy and its associated care by herself.

It felt wrong this way. Incomplete. As if something fundamental was missing from the picture. Like the father.

Her breath hitched, stuck in her throat, as it did too often when she thought of Alexios. Why did it still do that? Why did she still ache for him after what he had done? Why had he even done what he had done? It tormented her, kept her awake at night and uneasy during the day, trying to put the pieces of the puzzle together. What did her father have to do with anything, as Alexios had hinted, except leave her with the fortune Alexios was so determined to steal?

It was like a jigsaw puzzle with half the pieces missing, the vital pieces, so the picture made no sense. But her wanting to understand—needing to understand—made even less sense. Because what did it matter if she had the missing pieces of the puzzle? Would it change anything? Would it fix what had been so irreparably broken?

No.

It was driving her mad, this ceaseless worrying. She had to stop it. She had to forget about him.

She waited on a crowded corner for the crossing lights to turn green, impatient to get to the clinic. All these people around her, jostling her, as they shuffled their feet and rubbed their hands together to keep warm, and never had she felt more alone.

But at least today she would see her baby.

Twelve weeks already. It was hard to believe, nearly the end of her first trimester, but perhaps, more importantly, slamming shut a door where she could have quietly dealt with this on her own.

And while a termination had never been a serious option for her, somehow, taking it away was a whole new ball game. There was no going back now. She was one hundred per cent committed to this pregnancy. To this baby. And the knowledge simultaneously excited and terrified her.

The lights finally changed and the crowd surged across the crossing. At least she had her bursting bladder to take her mind off things. If the technician was late, she'd explode.

The clinic was only a couple of doors from here. Soon she'd be laid out on that bed and a few minutes after that, she'd be able to empty this overfilled bladder of hers. Bliss!

Even better than that, she'd have a photo of her baby.

She was reaching for the door handle when she sensed him—a movement behind, of someone tall, large. Someone that drizzled ice-cold slime down her spine.

'Going somewhere, Athena?'

Breath hitched in her lungs as every nerve receptor in her body screeched in alarm. Alexios!

How did he know she was here?

She wouldn't turn around. She wouldn't look back, forcing herself to keep moving forwards, her hand reaching for the door handle and escape, when his hand locked on her arm, a five-fingered manacle, and once again she tasted bile in her throat, reminding her of the day she'd thrown up outside his offices. The bitter taste of it incensed her, spinning her around.

'Let me go!' She tried to stay calm, to keep the rising panic from her voice. Because if he knew she was here, he must surely know why, and she was suddenly, terribly, afraid. His jaw was set, his eyes were unrepentant, and they scanned her now, as if looking for evidence, taking inventory of any changes. There weren't any, not that anyone else might notice, though she'd felt her jeans grow more snug just lately, the beginnings of a baby bump.

'We need to talk.'

'No!' She twisted her arm, breaking free.

'I've got nothing to say to you,' she said, rubbing the place where his hand had been, still scorchingly hot as if he had used a searing brand against her skin, rather than just his fingers.

'No?' His eyes flicked up to the brass plate near the door, to the name of the doctor in obstetrics. 'You didn't think I might be interested to hear that you're pregnant with my child?'

Athena flinched, the beginnings of a headache stirring behind her eyes. It was as bad as she thought. 'This has got *nothing* to do with you.'

'It's got everything to do with me. Do you think I would leave the fate of my child in the hands of anyone with the name of Nikolides?'

She was too shocked to speak, any residual warmth she'd been harbouring about her time with Alexios evaporating in the heat of his open hostility.

'Why didn't you tell me you were pregnant?'

'Because if I never saw you again,' she hissed, 'it would be too soon.'

'Bad luck.'

The door opened and a couple emerged from the clinic, happy and smiling and clutching a photograph between them as they bustled by, oblivious to the toxic cloud hovering on the doorstep.

Athena took advantage of the distraction and angled past, squeezing through the door before it shut.

Alexios was right behind her, of course he would be, but at least she was inside. He wouldn't make a scene here, surely? She checked in at Reception, aware of the thunderous cloud hovering at her shoulder, feeling his anger rolling off him in waves. What was that crack regarding her name about? What did that have to do with anything? She didn't want to know. She just wanted Alexios gone.

The waiting room was only half occupied, a television propped up in a corner playing a daytime soap oozing melodrama that didn't come close to what was happening in real time. People glanced at them as they sat down, and then looked back at their magazines and screens, too wound up in their own reasons for being there to pay attention to the newcomers.

He leaned closer and said low under his breath, 'How long have you known?'

She glared at him, remembering the excitement of her discovery, and of wanting to share it with him. But that was before...

She looked away, picking up a discarded

magazine from the seat alongside. Alexios was too close, too big, and he smelled too much of the man she once thought she'd loved, and the pain in her bladder was suddenly no match for the pain of her broken heart.

'It was never going to stay a secret. I was always going to find out.'

So he'd had his goons watching her? She turned and glared at him, lips tightly pursed so she wouldn't unleash and tell him how much she hated him right here in the middle of the waiting room, no matter how much she was tempted.

A woman called her name, and she sprang up as quickly as she could, eager for escape. He got to his feet behind her. 'No,' she said, but his eyes narrowed.

'It's my baby too.' His voice was low and menacing and it was no consolation at all to know that he was right.

She didn't bother to answer. She just gritted her teeth and followed the technician.

So she thought she could get away with not telling him? Alexios seethed as he folded himself into the visitor chair in the corner of the tiny room. He hadn't planned on being so confrontational, but seeing Athena again had flicked a switch in his head. She looked the same as he remembered, but with drawn, dark circles under her eyes. She was clearly not taking care of herself. The woman might be stubborn, but he would fix that.

Alongside him Athena settled herself on the bed, her responses to the technician terse and monosyllabic, her head turned away from Alexios as if to deny his very existence.

Tough. He was very much here and he was not going to be denied.

The technician peeled back Athena's shirt, baring her abdomen to his gaze. Such smooth skin. Such feminine curves. And that curve there, where the technician smoothed on some kind of gel—was that the beginnings of a bump?

It was impossible not to want to reach out his hand and touch her skin. He remembered the feel of it under his hands. He remembered the taste of her in his mouth. He felt himself stir at the memories and he had to clamp down on his libido. She'd told him she was safe and yet she'd let this happen—there would be no more mistakes. There would be no more secrets. He would make sure of it.

The technician looked at the screen, the transponder sliding backwards and forwards over her belly, the only sound the clicks of the technician's mouse.

'Can we see the baby?' Alexios asked.

The technician barely glanced at him. 'I'm just doing measurements first.'

'Why? Is something wrong?'

Athena sighed.

'Be patient a little longer, please,' said the technician. 'It won't be long.'

He bristled in his chair, unable to get comfortable.

'Can you tell if it's a boy?'

'Alexios,' Athena snapped, wheeling her head around. 'Didn't you hear? Be patient!'

He almost growled. This was not his world, not his domain, full of strange machines and people who weren't falling over to satisfy him. Full of a woman who would have denied him his own child.

'Besides,' she added, directing her comment to the operator, 'I don't want to know the sex.'

The technician nodded and Alexios wanted to growl again.

Finally the operator was satisfied and turned the screen. 'Here is your baby,' she said, making some kind of sense of the swirling scan by pointing out the heart and the tiny limbs, the even tinier fingers and toes, freezing the frame at one point where the baby put its thumb in its mouth, to print out a photograph.

Alexios was transfixed by the moving shadows. It was all there. The features on its face might be indistinct, the sex might be indeterminate, but it was all there.

His baby.

And something huge, something mind-bending and mammoth, dislodged inside him, to crash down what felt like a rocky mountain into the canyon below.

His child.

And suddenly he didn't feel purposeless any more. Suddenly he knew what the future held. For he'd made good on his death-bed promise to his father. He'd exacted his revenge and evened up the score.

And now here was his reward—this child—all packaged up in the woman who'd been the vessel of his revenge.

It was perfect.

'Things have to change.'

In the seat at the café table opposite him, Athena stiffened. She wasn't drinking coffee and she hadn't wanted to extend this uncomfortable meeting, but guilt had forced her hand. Guilt, and the look on Alexios's face when she'd glanced over at him staring at the screen. The look of sheer wonderment on his features, when she'd realised that he, too, had

a stake in this child. Even if she couldn't bear
the man. Even if she wanted to hate him with
every fibre of her being for what he had done
to her. Even if she tried to hate him.

He was the baby's father.

'What do you want, Alexios?' she asked,
rubbing her forehead, the headache that had
appeared the same moment as Alexios now
thumping behind her eyes. She supposed they
could come to some agreement on paternal
visits or shared custody. That was probably
reasonable. Fair. She sniffed. She could be
reasonable and fair.

'You're moving in with me. The baby will
be better provided for.'

'What?' The man was a fool if he thought
she would do any such thing. 'No way!'

'You can't stay in your apartment. It's too
small. The area is too rough. It's not suitable
to bring up a baby.'

'It's fine.' Okay, so she'd wandered the tiny
dimensions of her apartment and wondered
the same thing, wondered how far her mea-
gre pay would go in providing for a baby. But
this was a first-world problem, surely? Whole
families in other countries shared the same
amount of space. And the area might leave a
bit to be desired, but she'd never had a problem living there. 'I'll manage just fine.'

'You can't live by yourself. It's settled. You're coming to live with me.'

'I don't want to live with you.'

'You have no choice.'

'Listen, Alexios, just because you happen to be the sperm donor that resulted in this baby, don't think you can railroad me. I'm its mother. I have rights too, and I do have a choice, and I say I'm staying at home. *My* home.'

'No,' he said summarily. 'It's out of the question.'

Athena sat there, momentarily too stunned to speak. Was the man incapable of listening?

'I'll organise the furniture removals,' he said, already tapping on his phone.

She sprang to her feet and banged her fist on the table. 'No!'

Heads swivelled in the café. People stared. Athena didn't care if only it got him to listen. 'It's not your decision to make. *I'll* decide where *I* live.'

His phone still between his hands, he looked up at her, accusation heavy in his dark eyes. 'First of all you tell me you are safe, when clearly you weren't, and then you neglect to inform me I have a child on the way and do your best to lock me out of my child's future. I think you've made enough decisions for the time being.'

She crossed her arms over her chest. He made it sound as if she'd deceived him, as if she were the one in the wrong. As if she were the one who had to make amends. 'I won't live with you.'

'Sit down, Athena.'

'Why should I? Why should I have to sit there and be bullied into what you want? What about what I want?'

'You're right,' he said. 'What about what you want?'

'What?' she said, so surprised that she did sit down.

'If I sweetened the deal... If I gave you something that you wanted...' He left the words hanging as he leaned back in his chair, almost a sprawl, emphasising his broad shoulders and long limbs and taking possession of the space. Owning it.

As he no doubt thought he could own her. *Bastard.* 'I don't see how.'

'You never did get the fund established, did you—the one for your friend, what was his name? Loukas?'

She swallowed, the bitterness of her foiled plans still a deep, constant ache. 'You saw to that.'

'Maybe I can help. I can put the millions up. You will get your precious wing dedicated in his name. I will even make you the benefactor so I take none of the credit.' He paused. 'How does that sound?'

'It sounds lousy. You stole that money from me.'

'I stole nothing. You signed your fortune over to me.'

'You tricked me!'

He shrugged. 'The result is the same, I will concede as much. But my offer would give you the means to fulfil your wishes to honour your friend.'

She shook her head, thinking about all those nights she'd lain awake aching for his touch. Missing him. Pointless, futile, wasted nights. 'I didn't think you could go any lower, Alexios, but now you are really scraping the bottom of the barrel. Now you resort to black-mail to get me to agree to move in with you.'

'I prefer to think of it as an inducement.'

'Semantics.'

'There's no need to quibble.' He raised his hands palm up, a set of scales. 'What's it to be, Athena? Do you want that wing to honour your friend that you were so excited about before? Or are you happy to live with the disap-pointment of knowing you could have made it happen, if only you'd swallowed your pride?'

He made it sound so damn easy, as if it

wouldn't be all kinds of hell to have to share the same house as him, to breathe the same air and for how many months. And afterwards...

'So what happens after the baby is born? What then?'

'That all depends on you, don't you think? If you wanted to be reasonable, I'm sure we could work something out.'

Work something out? Yeah, she'd just bet he could.

She wanted to tell him where he could shove his *inducement*. Wanted to tell him he could take a running jump into somewhere rank and septic, somewhere like the swamp he'd no doubt crawled out of.

But she also wanted what Alexios had stolen from her before—she wanted to honour her friend and mentor the way she had planned, the way that could never happen without a massive injection of private funds.

And her modest apartment was going to be a squeeze once she'd bought all the baby gear. But move in with Alexios?

She licked her lips. Because if she agreed, it wasn't just her pride she'd have to swallow. She'd have to live in close proximity with Alexios. A man she hated for the way he'd treated her, and yet a man who could still stir her senses with just one glance. She'd sensed his eyes on her naked abdomen while she'd been on the examination table. Felt the laser heat as they'd traversed her skin, that discomfiting prickling, the cursed awareness of the heat in his eyes, stirring red-hot memories of an earlier time.

When their lovemaking had spun her world around.

When she'd fallen in love with Alexios.

Oh, no, it wasn't her pride she was worried about.

'I won't sleep with you,' she whispered, having to struggle to get out the words, but they had to be said, if only for her benefit.

He cocked an eyebrow as he leaned forward, his lips curling at the corners. 'Is that a yes?'

She sniffed. Thought of Loukas. Thought about the work he'd done all his life for little reward or recognition and how surprised and honoured he would be when the new wing was announced.

Her throat was dry, her mouth ashen. She looked up at the man opposite through watery eyes, knowing she had no choice at all. 'It's a yes.'

CHAPTER TEN

GIVEN MOST OF her furniture was only suitable for donation to charity, Athena didn't have a lot to move. Infuriatingly, Alexios made it even easier—all she had to do was give a nod or shake of her head and an item was packed or dispensed with in the next moment. Before she knew it, Athena was saying goodbye to her small apartment and finding herself installed in Alexios's luxury penthouse with its minimalist designer furniture and maximalist three-hundred-and-sixty-degree views over the city of Athens. Even her clothes and personal possessions had been unpacked for her, and now it was too late in the day to go to work, so she had nothing to do.

Nothing to do but rattle around his sprawling apartment.

In the quiet before the time she knew he would be home, Athena wandered from window to window, room to room. She had her own suite. A large bedroom, huge walk-in wardrobe and marble bathroom with a sprawling bath. A whirlpool bath, she realised, trailing a finger over the smooth surface of the stone. All to herself.

She returned to the windows in the living room and looked out over the busy streets below. There was a wide deck that ran along three sides of the penthouse, a lap pool along the fourth. It should have felt like luxury. She should have felt pampered and special. Instead it felt like a five-star prison. She wandered through the spacious rooms feeling—awkward. Out of place.

This wasn't her home. She didn't belong. Even her few favourite things—a brightly coloured Turkish kilim she'd bought on a trip to Istanbul, and a set of fragile glass tear vases from Chania in Greece—looked odd against the penthouse's super modern decor.

Put simply, she just didn't want to be here. And even though Alexios had made it plain that she was to make herself comfortable and feel free to investigate the cupboards and the kitchen and make herself feel at home, no amount of exploration was going to make any difference to how she felt.

She was only here because of the baby that grew inside her.

She curled her hand over the slight curve of her stomach. She was beginning to sense the changes now, subtle though they still were. The slight thickening of her waist, the heaviness of her breasts, and this growing bump.

In a few months there would be a child born. Would she still be here, in Alexios's home? And if she were, what kind of family would they be?

She laughed out loud at that, but it was a harsh, mocking sound that echoed around the hollow space. What kind of family could they possibly be after all that had happened?

But then, did she know what a real family felt like? For so many years it had just been Athena and her mother, and then her mother had died, and she'd been thrust back into her father's world, but always an uncomfortable part of it, on the fringe, as if they had never really belonged together.

As it was with Alexios now.

She sighed. And to think she'd once thought…

'How are you settling in?'

She jumped and wheeled around. She hadn't heard him arrive. 'Fine,' she said. *Just dandy.*

'Are you hungry?'

'No.'

'Would you like to go out for dinner later?'

The question took her by surprise. Not because it was an unusual question in itself, but because of what it implied. 'Um… look, Alexios. This me-living-in-your-house thing. It's not like we're actually shacking up together. We don't have to synchronise our watches and do everything together, do we?'

He frowned. 'Of course not. I just thought, we both have to eat.'

She shook her head. 'I think I'll go to my room. I've got some reading to do.'

'Athena,' she heard him say behind her.

She didn't turn around. She didn't want to look at him any more than she had to. It was way, way too hard to look at him and remember what he'd once meant to her. 'What?'

'I know this isn't what you wanted, but we can do it the hard way or the easy way. Your choice.'

She tossed her hair back, kicking up her chin as she turned to face him. Because she had to face him this time. 'That shows what you know. Because there is no easy way. And now, if you'll excuse me?'

What was her problem? Alexios tugged at his tie as he looked heavenwards. She couldn't

expect to raise their child in that dingy post-
age stamp she'd called an apartment. And it
wasn't just because she'd hidden her pregnancy from him that she was here—although
it was more than enough reason to want to
set her straight and make sure she didn't pull
a stunt like that again.

She must see that she was better off here.
There was space and comfort and a driver on
hand any time she needed to go out, and the
neighbourhood was a huge improvement on
the dead-end street where she'd lived.

Besides, she'd agreed to his terms, hadn't
she? He'd signed off on the transfer today.
Whatever funds it took would be made available, with planning work to commence immediately. He'd signed off on his end of the
bargain.

So what the hell was her problem?

The sky offered no answers, but the weak
wintering sun winked on the surface of the
lap pool, beckoning to him. He reefed off his
tie. Yeah, physical exercise. That was exactly
what he needed.

Something Athena was finding about pregnancy was that she could go from not caring
about food to being ravenously hungry in the
space of a dot. Embarrassing when she'd told

Alexios she didn't care for dinner. She headed for the kitchen to find some of the fruit she'd brought with her, hoping Alexios had gone out without her.

It was a false hope. There was turbulence in the pool, muscled arms windmilling. Alexios, she realised, swimming up a storm, powering through the water lap after lap. There was something mesmerising about the motion. Dark hair spearing through the waters, powerful broad shoulders and back muscles rippling, feet kicking as they propelled him along.

He stopped at the end of the pool, rested for a moment before launching himself out of the pool with a whoosh, his foot landing on the tiled edge before he stood in one fluid movement. Droplets rained down from the vee of his body when he sleeked the water from his hair. Athena was spellbound for a moment, before she blinked and turned away towards the kitchen. It had been like watching a god emerge from the sea, all powerful limbs and muscled magnificence.

It had been like ripping a plaster off a wound.

And he thought there was an easy way of doing this? Not a chance.

She'd known exactly how difficult it would

be. If she couldn't stop thinking about him—wanting him—in the two months they'd been separated, how was she supposed to stop wanting him when she was right here, in his house, witness to his near-naked body and hostage to her own recalcitrant hormones?

But he'd held out a way to see her dream to honour Loukas fulfilled, and she'd hoped she'd be able to harness her anger and find a way through.

This was day one and she knew she'd been mistaken. Because the memories would never fade while she was here with him in this house, when she so needed them to fade. She needed to keep her hatred for what he had done pure and undiluted, and unsullied by memories of how it had been. Memories of his body next to hers. Memories of him inside her. Memories that hurt like a physical ache for what she missed.

And it hurt so much that the pain of losing him, and having him so close now, sometimes seemed to hurt more than the pain of what he'd done to her. How did that work?

Hormones, she told herself, selecting an apple from the fruit bowl and sinking her teeth into it.

It had to be pregnancy hormones. She couldn't afford to believe it was anything else.

* * *

She was dressed and preparing for work when Alexios appeared in the kitchen the next morning. He paused when he saw her, and looked her over, taking in her stretch skirt, sweater and boots, doing a double take of her eyes. *'Kalimera,'* he said, pushing buttons on the coffee machine. 'Did you sleep well?'

'Yes, thank you,' she lied. Because it wasn't the plush bed's fault that she'd lain awake half the night. For two months she'd slept alone and she'd come to accept that Alexios no longer had a place in her bed. For two months she'd told herself she liked having her bed all to herself again and that she didn't miss him and that she'd better get used to the fact she'd be sleeping alone from now on. But that wasn't when he was lying asleep and no doubt naked in the very next room. And even though they were very big rooms, there wasn't enough distance between them. Her body knew he was there, and it was enough to make her long for what was lost. Pointless longing, when the only reason she was here was this baby. Pointless, when he'd only ever wanted her for her fortune. Never for her. Not then. Not now.

Nothing had changed but this damned— *cursed*—proximity.

The machine hissed and spat as he leaned his hip against the stone bench and watched what she was doing, watched her put a pot of yoghurt and some grapes in the lunch box on the bench before her. It was unsettling. Unnerving. 'Maybe you should take the day off.'

'I had yesterday off. I have work to do.'

'You look tired. Moving was too much. You should be resting.'

'I'm fine.'

'You don't need to work now.'

She turned to him, wishing he didn't look so just-showered-fresh, the ends of his thick hair still beaded with moisture, his crisp white shirt just that tiny bit translucent, so just like that first day she could see, if she looked, the dark shadows... *No.*

'Yes, I actually do need to work. It's my job, Alexios. It's what I do.'

'But is it wise? Should you be working, in your condition?'

She closed the lid on her lunch box hard, but the resulting snap was nowhere near as therapeutic or emphatic as she'd hoped. 'Don't be ridiculous. I'm having a baby. I'm not sick.'

'You're having my baby.'

'And mine!'

'But—'

'Giving up work was never part of our deal, Alexios, and it's not happening,' she said, not letting him set the agenda. 'I might be pregnant, but women are designed to have babies and get on with their lives in the process. So what that I'm pregnant? It's not going to change who I am and what I do. I'm not going to let it and I'm certainly not about to let somebody else tell me what to do.'

He shook his head, looking at her as if she were a recalcitrant child. 'Surely resting would be better for the baby?'

'What, and stay cooped up in this gilded prison all day?' She snorted. 'I'd go mad.'

He sighed and put his coffee down, rubbing his brow with his hand. 'Why do you have to make this so difficult?'

She picked up her lunch box. 'I'm not. I'm simply trying to make it work. Have a nice day.'

The heels of her boots clip-clopped as they carried her across the tiled floor. How many more mornings, how many more conversations like this would she have to bear? She might just go mad anyway.

'Athena,' he called.

She turned, expecting more instructions. A reminder to look right and left before crossing the road. An instruction to make sure she ate everything in her lunch box. As if she didn't know how to take care of this baby. 'Yes?'

'I was going to tell you last night over dinner, but that didn't happen—the funding for Loukas's wing has been formalised. I've arranged a meeting at the ministry tomorrow to talk to the officials and get the wheels in motion. I thought you might like to come, to explain the significance of the finds.'

'Oh.' She blinked. 'You've done all that already?'

'It was my end of the deal.'

'Of course.' She nodded, and felt a tiny kernel of hope that something good might come out of this arrangement after all. 'Yes. I'd very much like to be there, thank you.'

He stayed parked against the bench while the sound of her heels on the tiles receded. He heard the front door snick shut and the whirr of the elevator motor.

He hadn't expected to ever see her again, but here she was, living in his house.

The mother of his child.

Pricklier than he remembered, more aloof, and with more backbone than he would have given her credit for. But still as beautiful. Her curves, her lush body, now growing more curvy with his child.

He'd expected he'd never see her again, but he had her now. He had her back.

'I won't sleep with you,' she'd told him.

He smiled. At the time, he hadn't cared. All he'd cared about was that she hadn't told him she was carrying his child. All he'd cared about was making sure she didn't pull a stunt like that again and keeping his baby safe.

But now he had her again. And being around her, watching her silken movements, smelling her all too familiar scent as she passed by, made him realise just how much he had missed her.

After all, she wasn't going anywhere...

It was so good to be away from Alexios's apartment and back in her office again, surrounded by her favourite research books and photographs of her at different historical sites and digs. After the modern minimalist decor of the apartment, it was comforting, like coming home and putting on a comfy pair of slippers. She shrugged off her coat and breathed in air that smelt like hope, discovery and the mysteries of millennia, and smiled. So good.

'Ah,' said Loukas with a smile of welcome, shedding his coat and scarf on the way into the office. 'You're back. How did the move go?'

She kissed her mentor on the cheek, and

gave him a quick hug, before she screwed up her nose. 'You know what moving's like.' And then she found her own smile, because she knew something Loukas didn't. 'But it's done, and I'm in, and it's very comfortable too, I have to say.'

He returned her smile, although there was concern too, adding creases to the corners of his eyes. He put a hand to her shoulder and gave it a squeeze. 'You are sure about this, are you? It just seems an odd choice after... Well, you know.'

'I know.' She licked her lips. 'But Alexios is so excited about this baby.'

And he cut me a deal... A deal he is already honouring.

The speed with which he'd got to work had taken her by surprise. And why? To make her feel more indebted to him? Perhaps he thought that. Although right now the scoreboard was so heavily weighted the other way, she was hardly going to heap praise on the man simply for doing what he'd promised.

The old professor nodded. 'Well, after all you've been through, I just hope it works out or he'll have me to deal with.'

And Athena laughed for what felt like the first time in for ever, and gave her old friend's shoulders a squeeze. 'Where did you get up to yesterday?' she asked him. Their jointly authored paper on the shipwreck find was due for submission to the archaeological magazine by the end of the week.

Loukas flicked open reading glasses from his pocket and fossicked around on his desk until he found what he was looking for. 'I like the changes you made,' he said. 'Once they're input, I think it's ready to send off. It should come out in their next edition.'

'So soon? Fantastic.'

'And I've had confirmation from the museum that we can use their amphitheatre to formally present the find to the public at the same time.'

'Oh, that's wonderful,' Athena said, knowing it would be the perfect venue and occasion to announce the new wing at the same time.

Loukas would get such a buzz out of that.

And that alone was enough to ensure she did her utmost to ensure her arrangement with Alexios worked.

Watching Alexios in action, dealing with a boardroom table full of politicians and bureaucrats, was like watching a master playing chess. Athena sat alongside him after she'd detailed the scale and importance of the discovery and others of the professor's career span, watching their faces, heads bobbing, pens flying, as he outlined the plans for the new wing. Of course, the 'free money' aspect was more than attractive, government funding being in such short supply, but it was the way he handled the problems the officials raised that impressed.

A new car park to replace the one overbuilt by the new wing? Not a problem. There would be multistorey car parking underneath, Alexios told them, with a new sculpture garden in the leftover space.

Troubles coping with increased visitor flows? Not an issue, not once the new state-of-the-art ticketing system was installed.

Problem after problem was countered, until in the end the group looked around at each other and thanked Alexios and Athena for coming, and said the group would deliberate and make their decision known soon.

'You were good,' she said, a huge understatement, once they got outside. 'Very good.' It was no wonder the man was so successful. He could negotiate the leg off a chair and get paid for his trouble.

'Don't forget your part,' he acknowledged. 'You had them eating out of your hand with your presentation. They can already see the hordes of paying visitors rushing through the doors.'

She blinked. All she'd done was speak from the heart. It was so much easier to do that when it involved her work. So much safer. 'Thank you.'

'And after all, we are offering them a fist-ful of euros.'

Now she was really surprised. 'We?'

'Well, we are more or less in this conspir-acy together.' And he followed it with an al-most smile.

Whoa! She had to look away. The last thing she wanted to do was to put her guard down and to start falling for Alexios all over again. He'd dumped her once before when she'd out-lived her use-by date, hadn't he? She had no doubt he could do it again. Probably was already planning it. For after the baby was born? Cast her out, her use to him as an in-cubator of his child negated?

After all, she'd trusted him once before and look how that had ended. She'd never be fool-ish enough to trust him again.

He glanced at his watch. 'Have you got time for a quick bite of lunch?'

She bit her lip, confused by the mixed mes-sages, baffled by her own conflicting emo-tions. 'I'm not sure…'

'It won't take long.'

His phone buzzed. He checked the caller, raised his eyebrows at her and answered. *'Ne?'* She held her breath as he kept his eyes on hers, watched his lips turn into a smile. *'Efharisto poli,'* he said, and nodded at her as he terminated the call.

She put her hand over her mouth, almost afraid to ask. 'That was them?'

He nodded.

'And... They approved it?'

'They approved it.'

And Athena squealed and threw herself into Alexios's arms. It took a mere moment, the press of her body against his, the scent of him curling into her senses, the feel of his big hands at her back, to realise the mistake she'd made.

She gave a little cough as she eased away, head down, unable to look him in the eyes. 'That's great,' she said, shoving her hands in her coat pockets so they wouldn't get her in trouble again. 'Really great.'

'So...' he said. 'Lunch?'

Given she'd just made a complete fool of herself, she wasn't sure it was a good idea, but after his support for the new wing it would have been churlish to say no. 'A quick bite, then, sure.'

A stiff wind had picked up, convincing

leaves to part company with their trees, and rain down in flurries on the pedestrians and traffic below. Alexios took her arm, as if he thought she might blow away with them. Her whole body tingled with the proximity, and with the heat she could feel through the fabric of their coats. He felt solid and strong and she so wished he didn't, but she still left it there.

If only to analyse the feeling and work out how she could let it happen. This was Alexios, the man who had betrayed her.

The man she hated.

But he was also Alexios, the father of her child.

The man she'd once loved.

And she'd never felt more confused in her life.

'How was your check-up?' asked Loukas, when she got back to the office.

She smiled at the little white lie she'd had to tell him, and at a secret wish that was fast becoming a reality. 'Brilliant,' she said. 'Couldn't be better.'

CHAPTER ELEVEN

IT WAS INCREASINGLY hard for Athena to remain completely aloof from Alexios after that. There were plans to be drawn up, plans he'd asked her to be involved with as specialist adviser to the architects, and he was always seeking her advice about one thing or another, more often than not acting on it. The edges of her resentment began to fray, the hatred she'd felt for him after his betrayal becoming diluted. This was a different Alexios, one who listened and who treated her as an equal—at least on this one project.

Meals were more often shared now than not. Conversations were less snippy, the new wing providing a neutral topic for discussion, and interactions were civilised. Even Alexios's attempts to micromanage her pregnancy had ceased.

But in some ways that just made living with Alexios harder. There was an underlying sizzle of electricity that seemed to crackle in the air every time they were together, every time their eyes met, every time he smiled.

But she wouldn't make the mistake of touching him again. Control was her shield. She was merely the mother of his child, was her mantra.

And every day, her baby grew and her body changed, her belly now sporting a discernible baby bump, the curve low and round, which was beginning to present a problem…

She was in her bedroom trying on clothes, but nothing in her dressing room fitted properly. She had nothing suitable to wear to the gala announcement, which was in two days' time.

Nothing from her old wardrobe was anywhere near dressy enough, and the beaded silver gown that hung in her closet and that she'd worn to dinner with Alexios that night—the night he'd said she looked like a mermaid and she'd ended up sprawled on his office desk—was now too tight. There was no way she could squeeze her breasts into the bodice, the skirt stuck over her hips. That was a good thing, she told herself as she battled to undo the zipper the scant few inches she'd managed to pull it up. She didn't need a memory like that in her head while she wore it. Besides, that had been the night before everything had gone pear-shaped.

The zipper was stuck. She'd tried to force it too high. Damn. She twisted and pulled for another five minutes and only managed to snag the fabric further. *Double damn.*

Alexios arriving home and calling out a greeting was the icing on the cake. 'Where are you?' he called.

She sighed. She had no choice. She was going to have to ask for his help. 'In my dressing room. I'm stuck.'

His voice came closer, from her bedroom this time. 'Can I come in?'

'You'll have to. I can't get out of this dress.'

She crossed her arms over her chest to at least keep that covered as he appeared through the door. 'What are you doing?'

'Trying to find something to wear to the gala. But nothing fits and now the zipper's stuck.' She swallowed. 'Can you help?'

If he said no, she was stuck. But if he said yes...

There was a spark in his eyes that lit a flame that warned her that maybe this wasn't a good idea, that maybe, if she just persisted with the zipper for a little while longer— 'Of course,' he said, coming closer, and if she wasn't mistaken his voice had gone down an octave, his words strumming a silken strand of web that vibrated between them.

At the last moment she turned around. Closed her eyes. Held her breath.

She felt his fingers brush her skin in the small of her back and her thighs clenched tight against the sensations stirring between.

'Isn't this the dress you wore—?'

'Yes.'

'Wow,' he said, and she could feel him tugging at the zipper, feel his warm breath on her skin. Her feet wanted to run. Away. Anywhere. Oh, God.

'It's amazing what a difference an inch or so makes,' she said, trying to sound unaffected and as if she weren't vibrating so hard with nervous tension she would any moment melt into a puddle on the floor.

'I had no idea.'

'How's that zip coming?' There was no concealing the note of panic in her voice this time. Her entire naked back was bared to him and she could just about feel his eyes raking over her skin, taking inventory of any changes.

'It's tricky,' he said, and she got the impression he was in no hurry, that he was enjoying the task much more than he should have been. 'I don't want to tear the fabric.'

'Forget the fabric!'

'Hold on.' There was unexpected humour in his voice but thankfully a tiny movement in the zipper, his warm fingers placed either side of her spine as he encouraged it free. 'There you go,' he said, sliding it down. Way down.

'Thank you,' she said, clutching the gown to her as she spun around and out of his reach before he got a view of what little underwear she was wearing. 'I appreciate it.' She was breathing hard now, waiting, but infuriatingly the man didn't seem the least inclined to go.

'Athena,' he said, his voice a low growl that purred down her spine, and she noticed the spark in his eyes had combusted into a slow-burning flame.

She shook her head. 'No,' she warned, even as every cell in her body screamed yes.

He rose to his feet, the excruciatingly long, slow way, his heated eyes imploring. She knew what she would get if she said yes. She knew what he promised. Exquisite pleasure and sexual, sensual gratification, her every carnal desire satisfied, her every now aching nerve ending instead lit up with pleasure.

But she knew what it would cost her too. It had taken the best part of two months to put herself back together last time, and she was still fragile. She couldn't go through that one more time. She couldn't be abandoned again.

'You had your chance with me,' she said. 'And then you betrayed me and you tossed me to the wolves. I won't let you do that to me again.'

She might as well have thrown a bucket of icy water at him, the change so dramatic, so complete, a cold mask freezing his features, the flames in his dark eyes extinguished.

'Excuse me,' he said. And he left her alone.

She sagged bonelessly into a chair, breathless and panting. She'd told him when she'd agreed to this deal that she wouldn't sleep with him, but now she didn't trust herself to believe it.

She didn't leave her room for a long while, using the time to sort her clothes, packing away those that were already too small. She'd have to go shopping soon to buy some more essentials but where she was going to find a gown at short notice, she didn't know. She'd have to try to get out in her lunch hour tomorrow.

She heard voices outside. Women's voices amidst Alexios's deep tones, and then came another knock on her door. 'I have the designer, Katerina Kolvosky, here with some assistants. She's brought you some gowns to try on.'

A woman glided in, age indeterminate though exquisitely groomed, full of smiles and congratulations as she and her attendants buzzed around Athena with tape measures and pots of herbal tea, while racks of designer gowns were wheeled in.

'Come, come,' Madame Kolvosky said, 'take your clothes off, my dear. We need to get to work.'

Two hours and two dozen dresses later, Athena's head was spinning, but she had a dress to wear to the gala. A dress the rose-gold colour of orichalcum itself, that paid homage to the ancient world, gathered over one shoulder and at the waist before falling in graceful pleats to the floor. A dress that was modest but feminine, that neither hid nor accentuated her baby bump. It was perfect.

And when Madame Kolvosky and her team had finished accessorising and clucked and tutted and wheeled their way out, and she took herself to the kitchen to fix something to eat, she saw Alexios emerging from the pool, his chest heaving, as if he'd just spent the last two hours swimming laps.

'Did you find something?' he said, from the door to the deck.

'Yes. I did. Thank you.'

He shook his head, shaking droplets from

his hair, droplets that landed on his shoulders and arms and combined with others to form little rivulets that trailed down his muscled flesh. 'Don't thank me. Consider it an apology. For earlier.'

'Oh.' She swallowed, reminded of the feel of his fingers in the low of her back and the gathering heat between her thighs at his touch. How long could she keep this up, denying her body what it craved when she knew that, if she only asked…? 'Apology accepted in that case.' And because he was standing there with only a thin band of black fabric between them with a dozen beguiling rivulets heading south towards it, she fled.

He watched her go, wishing things could be different. Knowing they couldn't. He liked having her here. The baby had given him a reason to seek her out—an excuse—but it wasn't the baby he spent his nights thinking about. It was Athena, lying in the bed in the neighbouring room.

Did she think about him when she was lying in her bed? Did she remember their lovemaking as vividly as he did? Did she long for his touch the way he longed for hers?

It had been both heaven and hell to touch her. Her skin had glowed like satin in the dressing room lighting, and felt like silk. He'd felt her beating heart under his fingers, and he'd wanted to circle his hands around her hips and pull her close so she might hear his.

But she'd pushed him away. Of course, she had.

He'd hurt her. As good as crucified her. He'd used her and betrayed her for his own ends. *The sins of the father...* That had been his justification. His excuse.

But she'd been an innocent all along. Guilty of nothing more than being the daughter of a man he'd sworn to get even with.

What kind of man did that make him? When all was said and done, was he any better than her father?

Was it any wonder she didn't trust him now? That she rejected his advances?

He burned for her. Dreamt about her. Was tortured by not being able to touch her every single day.

So how was this arrangement to share his apartment and live together supposed to work? Because it turned out she'd been right all along. There was no easy way to do this.

The archaeological magazine had a big splash on the discovery of the shipwreck and its precious cargo, not only publishing the paper, but photographs of the team on site, and of Athena and Loukas with the stack of orichalcum ingots recovered. Before long, the article had been syndicated to a dozen online news agencies and flashed around the world.

Athena was already in a sparkling mood before she hit the hairdresser, her hair styled into a regal up-do, her make up bolder, more striking, than she'd ever usually wear, but when she donned the gown and shoes, it all went together perfectly.

'You look like a goddess,' declared Alexios when she appeared, and the heated look in his eyes made her toes curl. She felt like a goddess, or as close as she would ever get, and nothing was going to spoil her good mood, not when the best was yet to come.

The big space was set up like a ballroom, with round tables for dining set between exhibits, a podium at one end and a dance floor. A string quartet played chamber music to one side as the guests entered and mingled.

'Loukas,' she called across the sea of shifting heads. He turned and made his way over, smiling at her, casting a wary eye over her partner.

'You look wonderful, tonight, Athena,' he said, kissing her cheek. 'And you must be Alexios?'

Beside her Alexios nodded, holding out his hand. 'Loukas.'

The pair shook hands and Athena got the distinct impression that Loukas was sizing the other man up, his eyes sharp and perceptive and more like a warning than any greeting. Then he turned back to Athena, his eyes suddenly warm again. 'It seems we're on the top table. Imagine that for a couple of dusty archaeologists. This way.'

'Imagine,' she said, and the smile she sent Alexios was as heartfelt as it was unwise. Because his lips curled and he winked at the shared secret, and sensation sizzled down her spine. She cursed as he put his hand to the small of her back to guide her through the tables and the spine tingles continued, and she cursed again that she was not stronger, that she could not turn off this desire for Alexios like turning off a tap.

Dinner proceeded, the chatter at the table full of today's headlines in magazines and articles, before the plates were cleared away and the formalities got under way. Speeches followed. A short film recording the discovery, commentary from team members excited to be part of such a find. Then it was Loukas's time to say a few words, thanking the team and the gods for the opportunity to uncover such a trove. He sat down to great applause, the MC announcing Athena as the next speaker.

'What's going on?' said Loukas, looking at the paper at his place setting. 'That's not on my programme.'

She patted him on the shoulder as she rose. 'You'll see.'

Heads from a score of tables turned her way as she started her speech, announcing the construction of a new wing on this very museum to display the treasures recovered from the shipwreck in all their glory, a new wing that that would be dedicated to Professor Loukas Spyrides, a man who had devoted his entire life to the pursuit of Greece's ancient past, a man who had overseen arguably the greatest discovery in modern times, and who deserved this honour like no other.

Loukas was crying, she could see, the tears streaming unashamedly from his eyes, mixed with smiles, mixed with hugs from those around him, flashes from cameras going off all over. Her gaze swept the table, landing on Alexios as she headed from the podium.

'Bravo,' he mouthed, and something shifted inside her, something she knew would never quite fit back in place again.

* * *

'I've never seen Loukas so happy,' she said, in the back of the limousine on their way home. 'He had no idea. He actually whispered to me, wondering what all those dreary politicians were doing on our table. How could I tell him?'

Street lights splashed mottled light against the windows of the car. The night had grown cold, rain lashing at the windows, but it was a night for celebration and Athena was still fizzing with the success of the night too much to feel cold. Fizzing with the thrill Loukas had experienced. Fizzing with being next to this man all night. So close and yet so far.

And suddenly it felt too far.

He wanted her, she knew from that night he'd helped her with her zip. She knew from every heated glance and every secret smile he sent her way. She knew from the crackle of the air around them when they were together. Like now, in this car, almost alone. The air seemed to shimmer with expectation, and she was hostage to it, just as she was hostage to the knowledge that she wanted Alexios too.

No. Didn't just want him. Loved him.

Her breath caught in her throat, a little half-hitch, the way it used to do when she thought about Alexios before he was back in her life.

But if she couldn't admit such a thing on a magical night like tonight, she could never be honest with herself.

'You did a wonderful thing,' Alexios said, 'honouring your friend that way.'

She slipped her hand into his, needing his touch, relishing the warmth of his fingers against hers.

'You're the one paying for it.'

He looked down at their clasped hands, clearly surprised that she had reached out to him, but he didn't take his hand away. 'I think we both know that's not true.'

'It makes no difference,' she said. 'It happened, however it happened. And that's the most important thing.'

Beside her he shifted, angling himself towards her. He squeezed her hand. 'I have never met anyone as selfless as you, Athena. After what I did…'

He didn't have to say it. She knew what he'd done. 'Can we not talk about that tonight? Can we not be adversaries for once?'

She took his hand to her mouth and pressed the back of it to her lips. 'I don't want to feel sad on such a night.'

His voice, when it came, sounded as if it were grated from orichalcum itself. 'What do you want?'

'I think—I mean, I do…' She smiled, feeling her heart tripping over itself, a drumbeat of encouragement. 'I want you to make love to me.'

Alexios was torn apart. Here was another of those requests he wouldn't ordinarily refuse.

Asked to make love to a woman he had hungered after since the day she walked into his life, the woman who was now carrying his child, should be a no-brainer.

Until now.

Because he knew in this moment with her hand held in his that what he wanted wasn't just one night of sex, or two, or however many. He wanted Athena in his life, and permanently. And it couldn't happen, not until he told her everything. Not until she understood why he had done what he had done.

'Do you know how hard it's been,' he said, his voice thick with want, 'to have you share my apartment, to have you within reach and yet not be able to touch you or pull you into my arms?'

She blinked up at him, the tiniest of creases between her brows as her eyes searched his.

He found a smile. 'I want to make love to you, Athena, but I want this time for it to be right—perfect—and the only way that can happen is for there to be no more secrets between us.'

His eyes beseeched hers for understanding. He couldn't believe he was asking her to wait for him. It was all kinds of madness and he was risking everything he held precious. Why had it taken him so long to work out what was precious?

But she'd told him she loved him once, and the only way she could possibly love him again was if he were to bare his soul and speak the truth. 'There's somewhere I have to show you first. Something I have to tell you. Will you come with me?'

She looked afraid, her bottom lip trembling, and he put up the pads of his fingers to still it. She kissed his skin, a whisper of air, a butterfly kiss. 'All right,' she whispered against his fingers. 'I'll come.'

CHAPTER TWELVE

EVEN UNDER A cloud-scudded sky, Argos appeared as a jewel in a turquoise sea. Athena recognised it when it came into view, feeling a stab of sorrow for the past, and for the father who wouldn't be there on the island to welcome her this time, even if he'd handed her over to the care of the housekeeper a scant ten minutes later and disappeared into the rabbit warren that was his island home.

Why had Alexios brought her here? He'd been so strange last night, so fervent. He'd left her at her bedroom door with a whispered *kalispera* and the brush of his cheek against hers, before leaving her restless and yearning. Whatever was troubling him, whatever he'd wanted to tell her was of such magnitude that he could not tell her then. But what was so special about this island? What did Argos have to do with anything?

It didn't matter. She wouldn't let it. Whatever Alexios thought she had to know, she'd already made up her mind. She loved him. She hadn't been able to stop loving him so she was hardly going to stop now.

And then, afterwards, when he'd said his piece, they would make love.

Beside her, Alexios pointed out of her window. 'Argos,' he said, shouting to be heard over the rotors, and she nodded back, feeling her past and present collide.

A few minutes later, they were down. 'It's so strange to be back,' she said as he handed her out of the helicopter and they ducked together low under the blades, heading for the herb-lined path. It had rained earlier and the scent of oregano and thyme hung on the air.

'Have you been here often?'

She smiled, remembering. 'A few times. My mother would send me to Greece for school holidays. My father would bring me here. I hated it.'

'Why?'

'Because I was just a kid and I wanted to stay at home with my friends, not be stuck on what I thought was an island in the middle of nowhere. Even if it was in Greece. To me the plane ride by myself from Melbourne was more exciting.'

'But you had your father when you were here?'

'Not really. He didn't know what to do with a child. He expected the staff to entertain me. Besides, he was too busy.'

'Working?'

'That, and entertaining his latest mistress. He had enough of them. This island was his plaything, as were they.' They reached the bridge over the pool, and Athena stopped, taking in the full view of the building. 'There it is, the mausoleum.'

'Why do you call it that?'

'Because it's so cold inside.' She shrugged as she looked around her, before letting her gaze settle on the man who'd brought her here. 'So, Alexios, why did you bring me here? What did you want to tell me?'

Alexios had been waiting for just that question. Dreading it. He gave a rueful smile and gestured towards an outdoor setting further along the patio near the pool. 'Come and sit down.'

The housekeeper met them with a tray of coffee, iced water and olives. Alexios thanked her and worked out where to start his story. 'It's about why I did what I did to the Nikolides Group—and to you.'

She shook her head. 'Do I want to hear this? You wanted the money. The lawyers told me to look out for people like you. I should have been more careful.'

'I wish it were that simple, but… Argos was not always your father's property.'

'No?' She shrugged, and he could see the confusion on her face. 'I guess not. So?'

'A long time ago, Argos had belonged to an old fisherman, a distant cousin of my mother, and who was moving to Australia to be looked after in his retirement by his recently emigrated family. The fisherman had offered Kostas, my father, the island for a good price, but still too much for a lowly villager to afford, even a lowly villager with big dreams.'

'What dreams?'

'He worked hard in his village. Everyone did. He had dreams of a hotel that catered for families from their mountain village and surrounds, a modest hotel on the sea but one that would still seem luxurious in comparison to their harsh village existence, with the potential over time for the hotel to grow, and become something larger. Something more.'

She nodded. 'Sounds fair. What happened?'

'My father reached out to an old friend, who'd grown up in the same village before he'd headed to Athens to make his fortune. Surely he'd help out a fellow villager, my father thought. His old friend would be nothing but fair—they could be equal partners. So Kostas shared the opportunity along with his dreams.

'And that friend shook hands and agreed. Right before he went and bought the island out from beneath him.

'My father was still busy drawing up plans and telling everyone in the village about Argos, when the news filtered out that my mother's cousin had left for Melbourne, the island sold.

'And when he went to the city to find out what had gone wrong, because it had to be a mistake, his supposed friend set his goons on him, and all but threw him out into the street. "Some people are destined for success," he told him with his parting words. "And some people are destined to stay in the village."' His voice was becoming more embittered as he spoke. So filled with the poison that had pulsed for so long through his veins that it was impossible to quarantine and keep out.

'So Kostas returned home devastated, his faith in people and his spirits destroyed.

'My mother was diagnosed with cancer a year afterwards. My father had no money for treatments, no assets he could borrow money against.'

Alexios looked out across the stretch of water that divided Argos from the mainland. 'When my mother died, it broke my father's heart. He couldn't cope. He spiralled into depression.' He shook his head. 'It was the end. And on his deathbed, I promised… I promised him that I would break his so-called friend the way he had left my father broken.'

'But I still don't—' He heard her intake of air. Her long exhalation. He saw realisation awaken in her eyes. 'This friend,' she ventured at length. 'This friend was my father. Am I right?'

He looked into her eyes, dipped his head. 'Yes.'

'And because of what my father is supposed to have done—'

'He did do it.'

She took another breath, tried again. 'So let me get this straight. Because of what my father is supposed to have done, you orchestrated an entire fiction to get even—not just get even, but get even with a dead man?

'And yet all that time, didn't you realise, you were getting even with me, someone who knew *nothing* about this? Who was never involved?'

'It wasn't about you,' he said, the words grinding their way out between his teeth. 'It was never about you. It was about your father. It wasn't personal.'

'Of course it was personal.' She jumped to her feet. 'You slept with me. That was personal. You got me pregnant. That was personal!'

'Stavros cheated my father out of Argos island! My father took him a deal and he stabbed him in the back—he betrayed him, and left him broken. My father died a broken man.'

'So this is how you get even with my dead father? By screwing up my life? By making me pay the price for something he's supposed to have done?'

'Athena, listen to me. Your father betrayed my father. I lost both my parents as a result.'

'But you can't pin that on me! Do you think my father cares about your revenge? Seriously? Do you think he's sitting in hell applauding your evil genius?' She raked her fingers through her hair. 'I thought you were just greedy—money hungry—I thought maybe I could excuse you for that. I've met enough people in my life that are, but you're mad, do you know that? This is madness. I want to go home. My home. Get your pilot to take me home, Alexios.'

'Athena, please… I thought if I told you, you might understand.'

'Sure I understand. And maybe you will too. Because it was bad enough when I thought you were just greedy. Money hungry. Because my inheritance meant little to me when I'd never expected it. I hadn't been a billionaire long enough to use it. It was no real loss to lose it, and I thought I could almost forgive you when you made my dream for Loukas's wing to come true. I really thought there was a kernel of good in you.

'But I was wrong. There's no good in you at all.' She shook her head, loose tendrils of her hair flicking about her face. 'And the funny thing is, I knew I could never trust you after what you did before, but somehow you got my guard down enough to think that we might even have a future together.' She snorted a very unladylike snort. 'Thank you for putting my guard right back up.' She looked down to where the helicopter stood waiting. 'Have you called your pilot yet?'

Alexios reeled. He'd thought they could clear the air. Start afresh. So he'd laid his cards on the table and she'd flung every one of them back in his face. And now there was only one card left to deal. One card he'd been hoping to share in more romantic circumstances.

'Please, Athena,' he said. 'There's something else I wanted to tell you.'

She sniffed, refusing to look his way.

'I love you,' he said. 'It's taken me a long time to realise it—too long—but I love you. Please…'

She turned her eyes to his, and he saw a wealth of pain there, pain that he'd caused. 'Please don't hate me.'

'I don't hate you, Alexios,' she spat. 'I pity you.'

They didn't talk on the return flight to Athens. They didn't talk until they reached the tarmac in Athens and Alexios could tell her what he'd decided.

'Our deal is concluded,' he said, as he handed her in the limousine to take her to a hotel that would be her temporary accommodation until she could find a suitable apartment. 'I'll have all your clothes packed and sent over, and then I'll see the lawyers. You'll get your fortune back, I promise.'

'I don't care about the money,' she said as he closed the door.

'You should,' he said, 'for that one,' nodding towards her growing baby bump. 'It's yours. It was always yours and it was wrong of me to take it.'

She nodded as the limousine started off. 'It was wrong. Goodbye.'

Loukas took her in, only too willing to give Athena a place to stay, accommodating her in his tiny spare room while her old friend tried to give her space, trying not to fuss. It was no long-term solution, they both knew, but it was so good to have a refuge.

Not that there was any refuge from the storm of her emotions.

Why had she ever imagined it might work?

How could she have been so stupid not just once, but twice to fancy she was in love with the same man? Love wasn't for her. Abandoned by her father, tossed aside by boyfriends when she ceased to be any use to them—surely the writing was on the wall. She'd been a fool to think this time was any different.

She put her hands over the bump where her unborn baby lay. What could she tell her baby about his or her father? That he was a liar? A thief? No, it was better they never meet. Her child was better without him.

CHAPTER THIRTEEN

ALEXIOS STARED UNSEEING out of his windows. What had he been thinking, to come up with this plan and to keep on with it, even after Stavros's death? Why couldn't he have let go, the scores settled? All bets and deathbed promises off.

Why hadn't he walked away?

He looked up at the Acropolis, lit by a watery sun. The gods had decided Stavros's fate. It should have been enough.

Why hadn't he deferred to them?

Except then he never would have met Athena.

There was a double-edged sword. To find the perfect woman and then to lose her—and to know he had nobody to blame but himself. He wasn't surprised she didn't answer his emails or his calls.

But he couldn't stop trying either.

Dark clouds that matched his mood hung

broodily the sky. There would be more rain later. And then an empty evening to look forward to, like the empty evenings since she'd gone and taken their unborn child, and all the empty evenings in his empty life to come.

And it was no more than he deserved.

Athena was sitting alongside Loukas in his office, not only the paper they'd jointly prepared on the shipwreck, but a copy of the plans for Loukas's wing now framed and added to the collection lining the walls. The plans were proceeding. That was something, but even that wasn't enough to cheer her. Winter had taken hold in the last few days, and rain streaked the grimy windows, an old radiator battling to pump out enough heat to keep the office warm.

Her phone buzzed beside her on the desk. She swallowed when she saw who the caller was, closing her eyes against the first few words of his text, immediately switching it off and burying it in her jacket pocket. She should have blocked him. She would have to block him. And yet…

'Who was that?'

'Nobody.'

'Oh, I thought it might be Alexios.'

She glanced up at him, started to hear his name. 'Same thing, really.'

'What did he want?'

'To see me, same as every other time he messages.'

'And will you?'

'Of course not.'

'And still he keeps messaging. Why do you think that is?'

'Because he can't take no for an answer. Because I am having his child and he can't bear that for once he's not in control.' Because he wants me to thank him for the hefty deposits that were being made into her bank accounts. She shook her head. 'I don't know.'

'Perhaps you are right. And perhaps there is a another reason—have you considered that?'

She swallowed. 'What reason?' she said, her voice cracking.

'That perhaps he truly regrets what happened. Because he really does love you.'

She snorted. 'He's got a funny way of showing it.'

'Yes, it must seem that way. What he did was wrong. I am not excusing him. But from what I understand, what he planned was against the daughter of Stavros. She was anonymous, nothing more than a target to redirect his energies. It wasn't personal, at least, not in the beginning.'

'It sure felt personal.'

Her colleague reached for a jug of water, topping up both their glasses before removing his reading glasses and leaning back in his chair.

'Have you ever asked him what your father is supposed to have done?'

'He told me. But what difference would that make?'

'Alexios saw his father suffer. Nobody wants to see their parents suffer.'

'That doesn't justify what he did to me!'

'No, but it might help you understand why he was so driven. Rightly or wrongly, Alexios is not a man to turn the other cheek. He saw his father betrayed and mortally wounded, and he hit back in the only way he knew.

'But he is also a man who knows when he has made a mistake.' Loukas paused. 'He took you to Argos and told you why he did what he'd done. Why would he have done that?'

'Because he was proud of what he had done. I don't know.'

The old man shrugged. 'Or maybe because he wanted to lay all the cards on the table. To not go forward until the air was cleared.'

He paused. 'Did anything happen that night, before he took you to Argos? Did something change in your relationship?'

'Nothing,' she said. 'It was the gala dinner.' But then she remembered the limousine, and asking Alexios to make love to her...

She looked up. 'What are you saying?'

'I don't know. I'm an old fool, but maybe he was getting to know you. Maybe he was growing to love you?'

'I don't want a man who can do such awful things and then say he loves me.'

The old man nodded. 'I understand. But consider this, which is the better man, the one who never puts a foot wrong, who never steps outside the bounds of what is right in society and law, or the one who straddles that line more widely, but who is strong enough to step back, and admit his mistakes, when he knows what he has done was wrong?'

'But he deceived me. He tricked me. Why are you defending him?'

The old man rested one gnarled hand over hers.

'It is neither my place to defend or damn him. My concern is for you. Have you asked yourself why you are so miserable lately?'

'Because Alexios betrayed my trust! Because he hurt me!'

He nodded. 'Yes. But is it also because you still love him?'

She wanted to say no. She wanted to scream it out loud so that the entire world could hear. But she couldn't. 'Oh, God, Loukas,' she said, her grief bubbling up from a place deep down in her chest. 'But I don't want to love him!'

The older man sighed. 'I turned my back on love and I lived to regret it. I don't want you to make the same mistake.'

'That was under completely different circumstances. You can't equate the two.'

'True,' he acknowledged. 'I'm just saying, be sure with whatever you decide, because the last thing you want to do is regret whichever decision you make for the rest of your life.'

He watched her, letting her think about that for a moment, before he added, 'I know why you left him. I understand how devastated and hurt you must have been. But now that you've both had time to think about things, why don't you meet with him? Just once. Listen to what he has to say and then decide. Where is the harm in that?'

Every cell in her body could see the harm in that. She didn't want to meet with him. She didn't want to talk with him. She couldn't afford to.

Because she didn't trust herself around Alexios. He had a way of finding the weak spot in her defences. He had a way of finding his way through the barriers she'd put up to protect herself. He'd proven that once before. And the walls she'd hastily re-erected after his betrayal were untested, cobbled together from the ruins, the mortar between them still drying.

She wasn't sure they would hold. She wasn't sure they could protect her.

Loukas was only right about one thing. She was miserable.

But now he'd planted a seed in her mind that was rapidly growing into a weed to rival Jack's bean stalk. What if she had made the wrong decision and she regretted it and was miserable for ever? What if Alexios truly had wanted to marry her—not as one more part of his twisted plan for revenge against her father, but because he'd grown to love her?

She curled her hands over the curve of her baby bump. Her baby deserved more from her than that. Her baby deserved her certainty. If she'd done the right thing, she should be happy about it, not living this half-life she seemed to be living now.

But the worst of it was, there was only one way to be sure.

She sucked in a breath and pulled her phone out, called his number.

'Athena,' he said after the first ring, sounding strangled and breathless and desperate. She squeezed her eyes shut, her heartstrings pulling tight at the sound of her name on his voice. How much she had missed his voice.

'The café in Thera,' she said, willing herself to stay strong. 'The one where we met. Meet me there…'

He didn't argue as she reeled off the details as dispassionately as she could. She didn't expect him to.

But as she terminated the call, neither did she expect to find herself looking forward to seeing him again.

CHAPTER FOURTEEN

HE SWIRLED THE cup in his hand, stirring up the thick dregs that echoed the thick dregs of his own life, bitter and undrinkable. Except his life was no cup he could push away when he'd had enough. He had to wake up to twenty-four hours of them every day.

Except now she'd agreed to see him. That was good, wasn't it? She could have said no like the thousand times she'd said no to him before, but she hadn't. This time she'd agreed to meet him.

Why? What did it mean? He wanted to think it was good, but what if he was wrong? He couldn't bear it if he was wrong.

But then, maybe she just wanted to tell him to stop calling to his face. So he'd get the message once and for all.

The cold wind whipped up over the caldera, squeezing its way through the gaps in the blinds to find the gaps through his unbuttoned coat and scarf to inflict pain on any piece of exposed skin.

He didn't shift when the icy fingers found the gap at his throat or at his ankles. Pain was good. It meant he was alive.

Strange though, when the rest of him felt as if he were dead.

She could tell it was him inside. He sat in the café looking out over the caldera as a rain cloud scudded across the sea, his tiny cup of coffee dwarfed in his hands. His hair was longer, wilder, his jaw unshaven, and his coat not buttoned up, as if he couldn't be bothered getting properly dressed.

Oh, Alexios.

And even though she should be gratified he looked like rubbish, even knowing what he'd done—all the planning, the intent, the lengths he'd gone to—even in the wake of the anger she'd felt at his betrayal—the soul-destroying hurt—a part of her heart went out to him.

Why should that be so? Why wasn't it possible to stop loving someone on demand? Why did they still claim a piece of you?

It wasn't fair.

Her baby fluttered inside her, as if sensing its father was close. She put a protective hand over her belly, rounder now under the loose sweater and coat she wore against the winter chill. 'It's okay,' she murmured as the wind tugged at her ponytail. 'I'll look after you.' And she pushed open the door.

'May I?' she said, holding the back of the seat alongside him.

He turned suddenly, his dark eyes jagging with hers, bottomless calderas filled with a world of sorrow.

'Of course,' he said, and she looked away and sat down before they could read too much in hers.

'How are you?' he said, his eyes scanning her face before dropping to her belly.

'I'm fine.' She licked her lips as she pushed wind-blown tendrils of hair back behind her ears. She knew she had bags under her eyes and she knew it was all down to him, but damned if she was going to admit it. Not when it was so hard being this close and yet so distant at the same time. The scent of him made her want to lean into him. The shape of him made her want to reach out her arms and touch him. 'The baby's fine.'

He gave a sigh, and said, 'That's good,' while his long-fingered hands toyed with the tiny cup, and she was instantly reminded of how they felt on her. Warm. Knowing. So easily able to cause ripple upon ripple of pleasure.

She felt it now, and shivered against the sensation, pressing her knees together under the table.

'Would you like coffee?' he asked, and he gestured for the waiter when she asked for herbal tea.

A fresh Greek coffee for him arrived along with a fresh glass of water and her tea. She allowed herself a moment to appreciate the sight of him nursing the tiny cup, raising it to his lips, and sipping of the hot, rich liquid. She was almost jealous.

'You like your coffee strong.'

'It helps me think.'

'Thinking is good. But you also mustn't forget to smile.'

He turned his face to hers and blinked, and she could tell he was remembering too, and playing back that first ever conversation. 'I had something to smile at once, something so special I should have cherished it, but instead I destroyed it. There is little to smile at now.' His eyes scanned her face. 'Why did you ask to meet?'

She shrugged. 'I wanted to better under-stand. Last time was so fast. So hard. I didn't want to remember that as the last time we ever talked.'

He looked as if she'd delivered him a blow. 'I don't know if anyone could ever understand. I have no words that could make anybody understand. I was so hungry for revenge, I wanted to break Stavros—financially, mentally, any way I could. I wanted him to feel the despair my own father did—the despair that hounded him until his death. When Stavros died, I turned that hunger towards you. I wanted to break you.'

He looked away, sucked in air.

'I thought it would be easy. I imagined it would be quick, over in a matter of days. But I didn't know you then, and as our time together expanded, and the longer I was with you, the more I wanted to be with you and the less inclined I was to set my plan in process. I told myself it was so you would trust me more, and it would be all the harder for you when it happened. I actually believed it…'

He watched her face. Must have seen her swallow down on that unsavoury piece of information. 'I know,' he added. 'When the longer I spent with you, the more I wanted it not to end. When it finally did, I had to remind myself why I was doing it. I'd worked towards it for ten years. It was all there was in my life.'

'Are you saying I did mean something to you then?'

'*Theos,* yes, you did and you do. So much, no matter how much I denied it. When I learned you were pregnant, it was just one more excuse to get you close. To have you near again. Because suddenly there was nothing in my life any more. My life was empty. Until you came back.'

She sucked in air. 'That night, at the gala. I asked you to make love to me. Why didn't you?'

He shrugged. 'Because you needed to know, before I broke your heart again, what kind of man I am. Because one day you would have found out. And you would have hated me when you did, whenever that happened, and it would have been harder then. It would have been worse.'

She sat back in her seat, sucked in a breath, trying to digest all that he had told her.

'Ironic, isn't it?' he said. 'For now it is me who is broken, knowing what I did to you, knowing what I have lost. And it is no more than I deserve.' He swilled the rest of his coffee. 'Thank you for wanting to meet. It's good to see you again. You look…good.'

She put her hand to his arm as he stood. 'Alexios, wait. Don't you understand why I'm here?'

'To tell me you want me to stop calling you?'

She shook her head. 'No. Because there was something I had to tell you. I wanted to hear your words first, but my words need to be aired too.'

He sighed and sat down again, looking resigned.

'Because I wanted to hate you, Alexios. And I think I did—for a while. I hated you so much I wished the worst thing I possibly could for you.' She hesitated. 'At one time, I admit, I wished you dead.' He flinched at that, but it was the truth, and they were words he had to hear.

'But still you funded Loukas's wing, even after I'd gone.'

'How could I not, after what I'd done to you?'

She shook her head. 'I didn't expect it, that's all.'

'I promised you.' He paused. 'And I promised you, you would get your money back.'

She nodded. 'Thank you.'

He shook his head. 'Never, ever, thank me. I don't deserve it. I will never deserve it.'

She sniffed. 'But don't you see, it doesn't matter.' She placed one hand over her belly. 'What matters is us. I can never condone what you did, and I can't believe you ever thought it would make things right, but you're the father of this baby, and I believe you changed your mind. Because you love me.'

His features were anguished. Sincere. 'I do. Oh, God, Athena, I do love you.'

'And that's the crux of my problem, Alexios, because while I wanted to hate you, I still love you too.'

She dragged in a breath that smelt of the sea and salt and an island that would be here for ever, whatever disaster befell it. This island had started again, after a cataclysmic eruption that had failed to wipe it from the world, and now it was one of the most beautiful and sought-after islands in the world to visit. Could she and Alexios come back from disaster too? Could they recover and become something bigger too? Wasn't it worth a try?

'Could we start again, do you think?' she said. 'Could we try again, with no secrets this time, no secret agendas? Just love between us, and this child. Do you think we could make it work?'

His beautiful face crumpled. Athena had never seen a man cry with such sadness, but she witnessed it now, witnessed his tears as he nodded, his lips too twisted for now to speak.

'I love you, Athena,' he said, when his mouth had unclenched enough to speak, pulling her into his embrace. 'I love you for ever.'

She sighed as she felt his arms around her. It was the only place she ever wanted to be, and it felt good. It felt right. 'I love you, so much,' she said.

They kissed as the wind buffeted the blinds, whipping through the gaps, cold and hard, but it was refreshing too, in its iciness, tugging at the memories of what had gone before, ripping them away, to leave only what mattered most.

Love.

EPILOGUE

THE SANTORINI CHAPEL she'd chosen with Alexios to exchange their vows was small but beautiful, white-walled and blue-domed on the outside, an explosion of colour illuminating the inside. Frescoes lined the walls and ceiling, intricate carvings framing the altar, with tall gilded candlesticks providing the golden, flickering lighting.

The perfect place for a wedding. The perfect time.

Athena slipped her arm in Loukas's as they waited for the cue to make their entrance. He patted her hand and smiled at her. 'Are you nervous?'

'A little,' she said, though not quite sure if it was butterflies she was feeling, or the fluttering movements of her unborn child. She rested her hand over the lace of her gown covering her bump and smiled.

Their unborn child.

Hers and Alexios's.

Because neither of them had wanted to wait a moment longer to be married.

'Before we begin,' her mentor beside her said, 'there's something I've been meaning to say to you.'

Athena looked up, the look on her colleague's face so anguished, she feared for a moment that something must be wrong. 'What is it?'

He tugged at the unfamiliar shirt collar of his unfamiliar suit and gave a little cough, and Athena sensed it was emotion he was choking back on. 'I'm honoured to be the one you chose to give you away,' he said. 'You are the daughter I never had and now you are giving me the gift of a family I never had. I wish you a long and happy life with the man you love.'

Her heart swelled. 'Thank you, Loukas. There's nobody I would rather have with me on this day.'

He patted her hand. 'But that's not all. Because, I'm proud of you, Athena, so proud of all you have become and all you have achieved. And I know, this is only the beginning. You deserve to have a wonderful life.'

The lenses of her eyes turned smeary. Her teeth squeezed down hard on her bottom lip to stop the tears so close to being shed from escaping. It was the speech a father should give his daughter on her wedding day, the words her own father had never managed to utter to her face. To hear them at all was a wedding gift like no other.

She reached up and kissed his weathered cheek, delighting him if his chortle was any indication. 'Thank you for all you have done for me, Loukas. Meeting you was the best thing I have ever done.'

'Right now I'll settle for second best,' he said with a smile, as the music changed, signalling their cue.

There was a murmur of voices as they set off slowly between the gathered guests, heads swivelling. Just a few of their colleagues from the university, a scattering of employees from the Kostas Foundation, even two of her old friends from high school, who'd come all the way from Melbourne.

But it was the man waiting for her at the front who held her gaze. The man whose eyes drew her to him like the moon tugging inexorably at the sea. The man whose eyes shone with so much love, she felt a burst of sunshine light up her soul. And for one moment, she wondered why she should be so lucky to have found a man who could do that with just one glance. She wondered what she had done to deserve to be so happy.

She reached his side and he gazed down at her. 'You look beautiful.' And as she smiled back up at him, staring into his handsome face, it was only then that she noticed the faint sheen on his brow, as if the heating was turned up too high against the outside's winter air.

'I love you,' she whispered, and his hand squeezed hers in reply, before the priest began the ceremony that would join them as husband and wife.

Afterwards everyone toasted the newlyweds with champagne and ouzo at Alexios's Venetian palace, the terrace strung with lights that twinkled and swayed in the wind swirling over the cliffs, the waters of the caldera dark until the clouds parted, and made way for the setting sun to rain down its golden blessings.

It was hours before the guests departed, hours before Athena and Alexios were alone and could consummate their marriage in the time-honoured way. It was tender and slow. A time to cherish and worship. A time for their bodies to commit to each other, echoing the words they'd exchanged earlier.

'I was worried, you know,' he said, after their lovemaking, 'at the church, I mean.'

He was sitting on the bed with his back against the bedhead, her head in his lap while his fingers toyed lazily in her hair. Her scalp was humming at his touch, her entire body humming after their lovemaking. 'What were you worried about?'

'That after everything that's happened, that you might have second thoughts. That you might change your mind. When I saw you on Loukas's arm, actually there, actually walking your way towards me, it was one of the happiest moments of my life.'

'We weren't even married then.'

'I know. But it was in that moment that I realised I'd been holding my breath, just in case you decided you could do better.'

She took hold of the hand in her hair and squeezed it. 'But I would never have done that, Alexios. How could I do better than marry the father of my child and the man I love with all my heart? How could I do better than marry the man who is perfect for me in every way?'

He rested his other hand on her growing baby bump, over where their unborn child grew. 'I'm not perfect, Athena. You know that, more than anyone. Thank you for giving me a second chance. I promise to try, every single day, to be the man you deserve, and the father our baby deserves.'

She smiled, warmed bone-deep by his promise and his sincerity-laden words. 'I know you will,' she said. 'And maybe *perfect* was the wrong word. Maybe perfect is overrated. Because I know my father was far from perfect. I realise now he was ruthless and selfish and he hurt people along the way. But he was still my father, and I can't hate him. I'll never hate him. Not when he gave me the greatest gift of all.' She brought his hand to her lips, and kissed the back of it, the gesture of his that she had always loved. 'You.'

'Athena…' His voice was a choked rumble, her new husband's eyes blinking hard against the moisture that misted their surface. He gathered her up in his arms, half lifting her, half sliding down the bed, until they were body to body, face to face. 'God, woman, do you have any idea how much I love you?'

She opened out her arms to him in invitation, her lips curling into a knowing smile. 'Show me.'

And he did.

* * * * *

If you enjoyed
Consequence of the Greek's Revenge
by Trish Morey,
you're sure to enjoy these other
One Night With Consequences stories!

The Sheikh's Shock Child
by Susan Stephens

Crowned for the Sheikh's Baby
by Sharon Kendrick

The Italian's One-Night Consequence
by Cathy Williams

Princess's Nine-Month Secret
by Kate Hewitt

Available now!